THE HOLIDAY DOCTOR

After a hiatus of four years, Susan Vengrove returns with her family to their beloved holiday destination of Holland Green. But the village has changed — as has Dr. Gerald Adams, known to them as the 'Holiday Doctor'. Every villager appears to be hiding a secret, and Dr. Adams seems more distant, leading Susan to wonder if it's the passage of time or the fact that she's now eighteen. However, just as she begins to recognise her growing romantic feelings for the doctor, his own secret surfaces — he has a fiancée . . .

JANE LESTER

◆

THE HOLIDAY DOCTOR

Complete and Unabridged

LINFORD
Leicester

First published in Great Britain in 1970

First Linford Edition
published 2019

A catalogue record for this book is available
from the British Library.

ISBN 978–1–4448–4328–6

Published by
F. A. Thorpe (Publishing)
Anstey, Leicestershire

Set by Words & Graphics Ltd.
Anstey, Leicestershire
Printed and bound in Great Britain by
T. J. International Ltd., Padstow, Cornwall

This book is printed on acid-free paper

1

Susan Vengrove looked up from where she was kneeling on the bedroom floor, fitting the knitted dress on to Elspeth's skinny eleven-year-old figure. Fitting wasn't really quite the right word. Susan had knitted the dress herself because everything in the shops hung like sacks on Elspeth, but the child needed something warm for an English summer, and the summers she remembered at The White House in Holland Green hadn't been all that warm.

'It's not bad,' she pronounced, with a satisfaction about her own work that she didn't really feel. But it served to partly reassure Elspeth. A little of the built-in anxiety left the child's thin face. 'And this warm red really suits you. Puts life into you. Makes you feel warm. Don't you think?' she added, in the hope of a spark of enthusiasm from Elspeth.

'Yes, thank you, Cousin Susan,' Elspeth murmured.

Merida, from the direction of the wardrobe mirror said, in her languid young voice, 'I shall need some new clothes, of course.' Merida always needed new clothes, but then she could afford them. She had what amounted to a private fortune of her own, to say nothing of Uncle Damien's wealth, Susan thought, with a sigh. Not for herself, because she wasn't very clothes conscious. But it seemed hard on these children that there should be so little money.

Merida pushed back her honey blonde hair and accused, 'You're not listening to me, Sue! Put that hideous knitting down and look at me. Will that pale mauve suit me, that we saw in Palmer's windows? It's not really a mauve. It's called Orchid. I think it will look rather *me*, don't you think?'

Elspeth murmured anxiously to Susan, 'Is this dress really hideous?' and Susan murmured back, while Merida was still talking, 'No, she always calls things hideous if they aren't for her,' and Elspeth relaxed.

The door was wide open. It was Susan's bedroom so everyone came in and out. The boys came in at that moment, glanced briefly at their cousin Merida, trying out new make-up in front of the mirror, and gravitated as by instinct to Susan. Colin promptly sprawled on the bed. At ten, he was a big boy. He would be handsome when he was older. At the moment he was just big and clean scrubbed, with an over-bearing eagerness and confidence that tended to swamp the other children. His brother Frankie was only eight, very thin, rather like Elspeth, but not quiet and shy like her. Noisy, very noisy, with a high penetrating staccato voice that could be wearing, and a passionate desire to know what was going on, whether it concerned him or not.

He was worried, now, about the arrangements. 'When are we going to

Holland Green, Cousin Susan, when, when, when? I mean, what's it like? Will I take everything I possess or just an overnight case? I'm not packed ready yet. Cousin Susan, you're not listening!'

He leaned against Susan, peering round under her face. Colin took him by the back of his collar to pull him off, but he struggled, yelling lustily for Linda. Linda Percy, the other cousin, orphaned since babyhood, hurled herself in from where she had been balancing on the landing window sill, and came to Frankie's defence. 'Is it a fight?' she shouted. It was her battle-cry.

Susan got up without haste, pulled the three of them apart, said briefly, 'It's going to be a story,' and pushed them into sitting positions on the floor. She could always gain their attention like that.

Merida said belatedly, trying out a new pair of eye-lashes with great concentration, 'I advise you to keep that lot quiet. Daddy didn't like it yesterday when they were whooping about up here.'

Susan nodded. It was understand-able. This was Uncle Damien's house and everything in it was his. Susan had been brought up in this house. Her parents, like those of the four children, had travelled extensively, and when they had died four years ago, she had known she was to continue in this house, with a slight difference: she was penniless. They had left nothing, after the normal debts had been paid. Their recent ill-health had eaten up what cash they had had.

Susan said, 'Now, about The White House in Holland Green — '

' — which isn't nearly so grand as it sounds,' Merida put in.

Susan ignored her. ' — it is rather a jolly place because it isn't grand and it doesn't matter how much you whoop about because there's only Mrs. Boffin — '

'Who's that?' Linda demanded. Linda disliked new people on principle. It wor-ried Susan. An in-built defence mechanism, she recognized, but Linda was too young, at nine, to have developed it so much.

'The housekeeper,' she said, smiling, and sewing a name-tape into the back of the knitted dress as she talked. 'All round and smiley and comfortable — '

'Hideously fat,' Merida put in, admiring her own trim young figure in the mirror, and flinging a disdainful sniff in the direction of Susan who had always liked Mrs. Boffin.

'She's a super cook,' Susan said to the four young people hanging on her words. 'She makes chocolate cream cakes and meringue fruit flans and — '

' — stews and Yorkshire puddings,' Merida put in with a shudder.

'You don't have to come,' Susan said thoughtfully, staring challengingly across the room at her cousin.

'You know I do,' Merida put in. 'Daddy says while I'm only seventeen I've got to stick with you, though why he thinks your extra year should make all that difference, I can't think. I wish Mother hadn't died when I was so young. This family is the end! All the people you really need around have died and look at us — '

She broke off uncertainly before Susan's frown. There was that look on the four young faces, a kind of baffled look, as if they could feel the rush and onslaught of tamped-down grief about to flood them again and they didn't know how to deal with it.

'Mrs. Boffin will give us a wonderful nine weeks,' Susan said firmly. 'Elspeth, she'll fatten you up so you'll fill out this dress I've knitted, and you, Colin, you've never tasted the sort of steak pie Mrs. Boffin makes. And — oh, yes, I'd forgotten, there's Alf Dinning. He's supposed to be the gardener, but he does a bit of everything and he poaches, only you're not to tell anyone. It's what's called an open secret.'

She had caught their attention again. 'And there's a chemist called Inkpen — remember him, Merida? He was a sinister character. We thought he was a smuggler or something, and let's see, oh, yes, the General Store! That was a marvellous place. They used to sell everything and it smelt gorgeous — '

'Tell about the poacher!' the children shouted, so Susan talked, winding more wool, this time for a thick jersey for Frankie, who would probably lose his vest again as he had done last week, and caught a chill. They would keep catching chills, because they missed their home, that small part of the Middle East where their brief young lives had been lived out, in the shadow of the oil concerns, and where the sun was always paralysingly hot in the day-time, and woolly things to wear had been unknown.

Merida said, hating being left out, 'It *was* fun, wasn't it? Every year of our lives going to Holland Green. There's a lake, you know, and woods — remember Willenfield Woods, Sue?'

'Oh, yes, and what about that old house we used to go into to play, in Yoxbrook? It was an awful place, but fun. Why was it always empty and boarded up, Merida? Do you remember?'

'No idea,' Merida said. 'We used to

get very dirty, I remember, and that man nearly caught us once. Who was he? Did we ever find out? Lauretta would know! I wish Lauretta were coming this time.'

There was a sudden silence. Then Frankie said excitably, 'Who's she? Who's Lauretta? I bet she's like that maid we had in El Shabah and she was all mysterious and used to creep around at night and my father said she'd have to go only a man came in with a thing over his face and a curved knife in his hand and he was going to kill us all in our beds because he thought we'd stolen the precious stone from the shrine in the cave — '

Very quickly he talked, his words tumbling all over each other. His brother Colin got up and said succinctly: 'Shut up, Frankie,' and he dried up. Into the silence Merida said, 'Lauretta was my best friend. I wish she could come with us this time.'

'So do I,' Susan said heartily. 'It would be like old times, only she can't because she's abroad with her mother, remember?'

'She said she didn't want to go,' Merida said mutinously. She had always like the petite Lauretta, who was sophisticated and a little too knowledgeable about grown men, Susan had always thought. At fourteen Lauretta had been inclined to slew her eyes round to see if any man present was looking at her, and those eyes of Lauretta's had been frankly inviting, so Mrs. Boffin had said once, Susan remembered. 'There's a little madam, if you like,' Mrs. Boffin had said, to Mrs. Kimpster in the General Store. 'Inviting, them eyes of hers. She'll come to no good if her mother don't watch out.' And Mrs. Boffin never cared who heard what she said about anyone, whether it was complimentary or not.

'Anyway, your father didn't want her to go this time, Merida,' Susan reminded her cousin. 'I don't think Uncle Damien thinks she's a very good influence for you. Anyway, there's one person I haven't mentioned, but I'm sure you'll all like him,' Susan said, a happier note creeping into her voice, 'And that's — '

'The Holiday Doctor!' Merida, as always, got in first.

'Is he on holiday too? What's he called that for? Is he old? I shall hate him, I know I shall,' Frankie — copying Linda's 'hates' — stuttered excitedly. 'Anyway, who wants an ole doctor? We're not ill, are we? Well, I'm not ill, anyway, and I don't want to see any ole doctor and I'm not going to, so there!'

'He's young,' Susan said briefly, her eyes holding a remembering look. 'And he's fun. Merida fell and had to have stitches in her knee and I got sick and we thought I'd been poisoned, and Lauretta — ' Ah, Lauretta had had a mysterious malady that even the Holiday Doctor hadn't been able to diagnose, but Lauretta had blissfully enjoyed four days of attracting attention from everyone, and no less than eight visits from the Holiday Doctor.

'Does he have a name?' Colin asked bluntly.

'Why, yes, he's Dr. Adams. Dr. Gerald Adams,' Susan said. 'Only we only saw him at holiday times so we called him the Holiday Doctor.'

'I shall hate him,' Linda said calmly. 'Elspeth will have to go and see him because she's got glands.'

'And she's 'neemic,' Frankie broke in quickly. 'And she'll probably die like that ole woman's kid in the *soukh* in El Shabah and we weren't supposed to go there because you catch things and Elspeth will probably fade away just like — '

'Shut up, Frankie,' Colin said again, and bashed his brother's head with a cushion. Elspeth stood white and rigid, holding Susan's arm so that the grip hurt. Susan said, 'Don't take any notice of them — you know Frankie always says things like that. It doesn't mean a thing!' and again Elspeth visibly relaxed.

'Why don't you tell him not to say things like that?' Merida asked idly, then almost at once she turned, her mouth painted a mauvish pink one side and a curious orange the other. 'Which of these lipsticks really suit me?' and she honestly wanted to know the answer to that one.

'Neither, actually,' Susan said, answering that first, and to the other question, she said, 'It isn't any use ordering Frankie not to say something. You know that. It's better my way, I think.'

'Well, I shall go down and ask Daddy which lip-stick he likes.'

'I wouldn't,' Susan counselled swiftly. 'He's got a man with him and his secretary said — '

'It's the man from El Shabah,' Frankie said, his eye-lids batting very quickly when he had made a pronouncement which he knew would gain universal attention.

He wasn't disappointed. Merida and Susan exchanged a quick glance, and Merida said, 'What do you think? Is it someone from the Middle East?' and Susan said, 'Well, if it is, it's hardly our business, is it? If you want to know, I think it would be a good idea to get out the cases and to start putting things in. I know it's early to start packing, but books and things — '

'They'll only want them all out again,' Merida shrugged.

'Never mind, it will give us all something to do,' Susan said firmly. And while she helped the children to gather their things together, she thought of the Holiday Doctor with pleasure and anticipation. He was one of the few people who had looked at herself and Merida without boredom and exasperation. She recalled his very vital presence, and those kind eyes of his, but she couldn't remember the colour of them. At fourteen, unless one was like Merida's friend Lauretta, a pair of firm hands and a pair of kind eyes meant more to a schoolgirl with a sore thumb, a bilious attack or a broken limb, than the glamorous accoutrements that seemed to go with the film stars Merida considered so necessary to her scheme of things. The way his hair waved back from his forehead was a blurred memory, but she knew too well the way Dr. Adams walked, and she thought she could remember the set of his head from the back view. That was the last time she had seen him, walking down the path of The White House, and she had felt unaccountably an aching sense of loss. Four years ago.

Such a lot had happened in four years. Her parents had died and there had been holidays spent at school. But there had been so much more than that. In the Christmas holidays at home in Uncle Damien's house she had heard servants' talk and got a vague but none the less obstinately lodged impression that Uncle Damien's affairs were not always flourishing and steady. There were times when he came near to the edge, financially, and in those times he was bad-tempered, unapproachably so, and inclined to look at his encumbrances with no great favour. Susan, for instance, and the girl called Mary, who was a very distant cousin indeed, and who had suddenly married in a modest way and gone. A colourless personality, she had bothered no one, Susan remembered. She had been useful to Uncle Damien as a secretary. Useful to the housekeeper and anyone else who had called on her. Susan could hardly remember what she looked like.

And now Susan herself was eighteen and had completed her time at school. Merida was to go to finishing school, but nothing had been said, so far, about Susan. Meantime, she had slipped into the job of being responsible for these children.

In the quiet of the small hours, when a hoot-owl awakened her, she sometimes remembered the Holiday Doctor treating her as if she were someone important. He had said to her once, 'Susan, if you ever need help, come back to us, will you?' 'Us' meant his aunt and himself, but the aunt was a shadowy elderly person. Susan remembered only the kind eyes of the Holiday Doctor. Now she felt warm inside, to think they were going back to Holland Green for nine whole blissful weeks. They would be free from the oppressive portly figure of Uncle Damien, who didn't always like his own daughter around.

The next day Susan got out her photograph album and showed the children her snapshots of Holland Green, but they weren't very good. It had been an old box camera, and now, after a period of years, she saw that through the eyes of people who didn't know the place, they wouldn't be very exciting.

Linda said bluntly, 'Who's that funny old woman with curlers in her hair?' and Susan had to admit that that was Mrs. Boffin, caught at six in the morning coming back from the hen coop with a bowl of eggs and looking, as she had wrathfully told Susan on realizing that her picture had been taken, 'not fit to be seen'. Susan had forgotten how plump and untidy Mrs. Boffin had been, and how prone to wear old carpet slippers.

Behind the housekeeper, The White House looked what it was; four old cottages knocked into one. But it had been fun to live there. 'There are still four front doors, and the removal men kept getting lost and very bad-tempered, when Uncle Damien moved in.'

'It looks small,' Linda observed critically, and Merida, coming to look over their shoulders, joined in that remark. 'Wonder what it looks like now, since the Twinings have had it?' she mused.

'Who are the Twinings?' Frankie was at once put out and suspicious.

'A young couple who asked Uncle Damien if they could live there at a reduced rent and keep the place decorated,' Susan frowned. 'It was better than to leave it empty. Mrs. Boffin didn't want to be there all alone.'

'Are we going to live with the Twinings? I don't want to!' Frankie said feverishly.

'No, pet, the Twinings are going to visit relatives. They'll be away some weeks. It was the idea of the house being empty again that made Uncle Damien think of sending us there. Now, not to worry. It'll all be perfectly splendid. I've had such a good idea.'

They all leaned heavily on Susan while she talked, Merida noticed, irritably. It wasn't that she wanted any child to lean on her. She didn't. Frankie had been in the garden and his hands were muddy and there were twigs and leaves caught in his jersey, and Linda was eating chocolate without much regard of her slacks and clean sports shirt. As for that scared kid Elspeth, Merida wanted to shake her, and Colin frankly made Merida nervous, he was so big and clumsy. But she resented Susan's winning their affection.

'I'm going to have a programme,' Susan announced. 'Two special outings every week, all through our holiday, and the rest of the time we shall spend how we like.'

'Can we get as dirty as we like?' Linda demanded.

'I have to be allowed to go out on nature walks and collect things and I keep them in matchboxes and don't let them escape and I must have a bicycle and — ' Frankie tumbled over his own tongue and lost his way in the many requests which all added up to the word 'freedom'. Colin said automatically, 'Shut up, Frankie,' and narrowed his eyes as he thought about Susan's plan.

Elspeth said, 'Can I stay close to you, Susan?' and Susan nodded.

'Soppy girls,' Colin muttered, but Susan stared over his head at Merida, who remarked, 'I wouldn't mind betting the Holiday Doctor will be in and out of our house all the time!' and she nodded meaningly towards the unsuspecting back of Elspeth.

2

It was raining, the day that Susan and Merida and the children went to Holland Green. Steady, cold rain that made needles on the windows of Uncle Damien's second-best car, a big old-fashioned Daimler whose one virtue was that it was roomy for four children and three adults and plenty of space for luggage. Uncle Damien's chauffeur, who was also the male secretary and general factotum, was not very pleased to have to do this trip. He didn't care for Frankie, who kept getting excited and jumping up to argue with his elder brother. Elspeth was travel-sick and worried, which didn't help either.

They approached Holland Green through Quenningwell, and got a shock: at least, Susan and Merida got a shock. The chauffeur didn't know the town and found the traffic too much of a problem to contemplate, but the by-pass hadn't yet been completed, so he had to take the long and slow route through the town's centre. The older girls got a good view of a town that had changed out of all recognition.

Merida was to a certain extent pleased. 'It's got big shops now — how marvellous! And there are two cinemas — oh, good-o, we shan't be buried in the country after all!'

'And a hospital,' the chauffeur said curtly over his shoulder. He had no doubt heard all about the Holiday Doctor and the holiday casualties in Susan's and Merida's time and had no great hopes of a peaceful holiday with these four children.

They looked gloomily at the big new glass and chromium building with the ambulances crawling in and out. Susan was so disappointed, she could have cried, but Merida was thrilled.

'What's the matter with you, Susan? They're modernizing the place! Just look what they've done in four years

— I think it's marvellous. So that's what they'd started to pull down Bread Lane for, when we went home four years ago.'

Susan didn't answer. Elspeth looked anxiously into her face and wondered why Susan, to whom she was now pinning every ounce of her faith, should look so wretched. Something bad was going to happen, or why should Susan, who was so cheerful, look like this? Elspeth couldn't know that fear was gripping Susan; fear that among the changes, the Holiday Doctor himself might have fallen a victim. He might not even be there now. Susan herself was shocked to find that she cared so much. He was an institution, a pillar, a milestone in her life; as much, in his own way, as Uncle Damien was, and much nicer.

Out of Quenningwell, they lost their way. The chauffeur wouldn't listen when they told him to turn right at the crossroads. They had to double back, and so they approached Holland Green from the north, and from that angle, it was all new, too. Both Merida and Susan cried out in dismay, for where Bullen's Farm had been, were now rows and rows of tiny new houses; a whole section of them, almost a little town of their own.

'It's all spoilt!' Susan couldn't help exclaiming, and Elspeth clung to her hand in a dismay she didn't understand.

Frankie was talking nineteen to the dozen about a boy who had been cuffing a little boy and Colin was getting excited about an advertisement about a roller skating rink, and Linda was trying to open a window to hang out, when the chauffeur swung round a narrow turning and swooped down a lane by instinct and then he was suddenly on the Green. Old Holland Green was still very much the same. The estate of small houses seemed to have been erected without planning, on the end of the village, but here it was as it had always been. Holland Green, with the church with the pale green spire and the lych gate; the rows of shops with their out-dated lettering above them; Inkpen the chemist standing at his door; the General Store — flanked now by six other shops but still looking as interesting and as packed with goods — and on the far side, The White House.

That really drew a gasp from them. It was no longer shabby, but painted a really dazzling white — bricks as well as paint — and the old tiled roof had been denuded of lichen, which Susan thought was a pity. Even the front garden, with its bushes and weeds and its wild flowers, had been swept away, and a very modern looking patch of flag-stones with a tiny pool in the middle, had replaced it.

'Oh, boys,' Susan said sadly, 'I was wrong. You won't be able to let yourselves go, not if the inside is as spick and span as the outside is. Oh dear, someone's been cleaning the place up.'

Their luggage was unloaded and

bundled inside the house just as soon as the chauffeur could manage it. He had practically thrown the last case into the small hall when Mrs. Boffin appeared from round the back. She was, if anything, more fat than before. She looked at the children, and then at Merida, and finally her eyes found Susan. 'Well,' she said, 'how time flies. You've both grown up!' She nodded at Susan, but Merida, sizing her up as an ally, flew at her and hugged her. 'Darling Mrs. Boffin, do you remember me?' she cried.

'Aye, I do,' Mrs. Boffin said, with no great pleasure, 'the pretty little doll I couldn't trust an inch. And where's the other little madam?'

She meant Lauretta, of course. Susan could see, without rancour, that Merida and Lauretta had made the strongest impact on the housekeeper, the memory of them lasting over the four years. She said, 'That was my cousin Merida's friend. She hasn't come this time.'

'Ah,' Mrs. Boffin said, and making a swift deduction, she said, 'Then you must be Susan.'

Looking back on it later, when they were all in bed, and the sweet country air came tantalizingly through the open casements, Susan was aware of disappointment. She had somehow thought the Holiday Doctor would have come over to welcome them. He was still here. Mrs. Boffin had said so.

There had been so much to do. She had made one of her big high teas for them, but Elspeth had been too sick to eat anything. Susan had helped her to bed, with hot water bottles. 'Delicate,' Mrs. Boffin had pronounced, as if she feared that even her good cooking wouldn't do much for that one. But Linda and the boys did justice to the meal — Mrs. Boffin thought they were never going to stop eating.

And now, under the deep low roof of The White House, in one of the biggest of those low-ceilinged rooms, Susan and Merida lay in narrow beds covered with new arty-crafty covers; dark purple, against white walls. Cold white walls, with a trickle of silver leaves in 'drops' at the corners. The boys had bunk beds in another biggish room which was happily an orange colour with furnishings of dark brown and white, splotched with a sage green. At least it wouldn't show the dirt. The little girls had a slip room each.

Across the silence, Merida said, thinking, 'Don't you feel you ought to have that Elspeth in here with you, Susan? She might be ill in the night and you'd never know.'

'I had thought of it,' Susan agreed, 'but there isn't another decent room for you. Where would you go?'

'Oh, I don't mind,' Merida said airily. 'I can duck down in the little room Elspeth has.'

Susan thought no more of the suggestion until the next day. Elspeth looked ill with dark rings beneath her eyes.

'Well,' Mrs. Boffin said, 'I knew it! We'll have to be sending for him. Haven't been in the place five minutes, have you, and over Dr. Adams has to come and him run off his feet as it is!'

Elspeth looked tearful at Mrs. Boffin's retreating back. 'Is she always so cross?' she whispered.

Susan fought down the rising tide of excitement at the thought of seeing him again, and answered the child. 'Don't mind her. I expect she's got rheumatism or something. Let's be thankful that the Holiday Doctor's still here. I had an awful fear that he might have gone, and someone else come in his place that we wouldn't like!'

Mrs. Boffin could be heard downstairs, like a sergeant marshalling the troops. 'Come on, now, everyone — there's a job for each of you. I want things brought from the Stores — you, son — what's your name? Colin — that's right. You can do the shopping from now on, and watch your change. And you, Little What's-Your-Name — '

And so it went on. Frankie detailed to fetch in the eggs and Linda to sweep the backyard. Everyone, except Merida, had a job to do. Wasn't that like Merida, to slip out of the way when the chores were being given out? Susan smiled in exasperation, and set about shifting Elspeth into her larger room, and tidying the small room for Merida. It took all of the time until Dr. Adams came, to shift Merida's things out of the big room, before it could really be called 'tidy'. And then Susan heard his footsteps on the stairs.

Funny, how one person's footsteps are so different to another's — it took her back over the years, to when her parents had been alive, and she had been no more than fourteen, shuffling half-heartedly through exams at school, and living for the day when they would be sent to The White House in Holland Green. Other girls might go abroad with their parents, but this had been the ideal holiday place, the do-as-you-like sort of holiday. And here he was, at the door . . .

Perhaps her memory of him had been blurred, she thought confusedly, for it seemed like a stranger standing there at first. And then he smiled, and said, 'Well, Susan,' and that was just like the last time, except that his voice had grown deeper, a little less vital? She asked herself just what the difference was, while she pulled up a chair for him by Elspeth's bed, and introduced Elspeth and began to recount the child's symptoms. He seemed bigger somehow, broader. He filled the room, to her fevered imagination, yet it wasn't a small room. He just had the effect of dwarfing everything.

But he sat by Elspeth and held the child's hand and she visibly relaxed, and by the time the visit was over, Elspeth was his slave for life.

'Lots of rest,' he said firmly, when he got up at last. He smiled down at Elspeth. 'Is there something you like doing, that you can do lying down? Not too much reading,' he put in swiftly, as the child's eyes turned longingly to a pile of books by the bedside.

Elspeth did nothing else. She was

ham-handed at sewing, loathed knitting and all forms of handwork, and couldn't draw to save her life. Susan looked comically dismayed.

'Well, we'll have to think,' Dr. Adams said, and rubbed the child's head gently as he left her.

The White House had an exceptionally large landing. It had been an off-room, when it had been four cottages. Someone had, with imagination, put a tall window in, with a curved top, and a window-seat. Susan and the doctor sat down on it to have the 'little talk' about the patient. 'Where are her parents?' was his first question.

'She hasn't any. They were killed in the same accident as the parents of Colin and Frankie,' Susan said worriedly, and now that she was out of earshot of Elspeth, she told him about the background of the children. 'Would it be a good idea if you met them all? It *is* a worry, because I don't know them very well either. Colin's so — well, not exactly secretive, not exactly quiet, but it's as if a wall has been built round him. I don't know what he's really like. Frankie, on the other hand, just batters everyone with his personality, and he's a bundle of nerves, and far too energetic.'

And when it came to describing young Linda, with her hates, and her tremendous vitality, and the lost look that came into her eyes when other children talked about her parents, Susan felt particularly helpless.

'And what about you, Susan?' Dr. Adams said gently.

'Oh, me! Another orphan,' she said summoning a smile. 'Poor Uncle Damien, he surrounds himself with them. He's very good to us,' she added swiftly.

'I'm sure,' Dr. Adams said gently. 'You've changed.'

'Well, it's four years,' she said. 'So have you,' she added shyly.

He looked away. She got the impression that he wished she hadn't mentioned him. He said, looking out of the window, 'We've all changed, most of all Holland Green. You'll find it's different everywhere you look. I hope you'll all manage to get a nice holiday, all the same.'

After he had gone, Susan had the odd feeling that they had almost become firm friends, but somewhere between discussing the children and her remark about himself having changed, the situation had slipped and he had at once resumed his rather formal manner. She was crushed with disappointment. She had wanted to ask him things. He hadn't seemed a stranger, once she had got used to his changed appearance. But now it had all gone . . .

She went back to Elspeth. 'Well,' she said, 'what did you think of our Holiday Doctor?'

Elspeth said, 'He's nice. I liked him.' She added, as an afterthought, 'He liked you!'

'He always likes the people who are sensible and good in the sickroom,' Susan said briskly. 'Sometimes I think I shall go to a hospital to learn to be a nurse. What will you do when you grow up?'

'I'll stay at home and look after you when you come home from a hard day at the hospital,' Elspeth said earnestly, and Susan hadn't the heart to tell her that student nurses were usually expected to live in.

As soon as Susan had had her belated breakfast she went to Inkpen's for Elspeth's medicine, and to renew her acquaintance with him.

He, too, was different. His shop seemed a little smaller, more crowded, and he himself seemed a little more important and aloof. Susan said, 'Hello, Mr. Inkpen, remember me? I'm Susan Vengrove.'

He said heavily, 'Having already passed the time of day with the excellent Mrs. Boffin, I've heard all about you. You will be Susan, the quiet one, and we've only one cheeky little madam this time. What happened to the other one? It's a wonder I didn't recommend to her father that he chastise her more regularly. In trouble, that one will be, before she's much older, if she isn't, already!'

He would be talking about Lauretta, Susan thought with a smile. Funny, the way everyone remembered Lauretta.

'And this medicine will be for the sickly wee one,' Inkpen went on. 'Aye, well, it's good air here, in spite of them bringing factories and workers here, to say nothing of building their houses! Mind you, I've nothing against building wee houses, all new and hygienic,' he was quick to say. 'I've a mind that they'd be built further away from Holland Green, that's all, seeing as we have preserved ourselves since Oliver Cromwell's time. Even to the ducking stool,' he finished, glaring at Susan as if it were her fault that changes had come to Holland Green.

'Yes, I'm sure, Mr. Inkpen,' she said quickly, and went to look at his display of cameras and films while he disappeared behind the glass screen to make up Elspeth's medicine.

While she stood there, Alf Dinning

came in and asked for a drum of weed-killer. He glanced at Susan as if he had never seen her before.

'Hello, Alf,' she said, with a broad smile. She was honestly pleased to see him. He had never looked more like a gardener, she thought, with his corduroy breeches ending in knee-high gum boots, and his waistcoat with bits of raffia and twine hanging out, and a pair of secateurs thrust in at a back pocket. His skin was tanned the shade of old leather, and his eyes were a startlingly light grey against the dark of the tan. 'Isn't it a lovely day,' she added.

'It's Mr. Dinning to you, now, miss,' he said severely, 'seeing as I'm not just a gardener any longer. Standing for the Council, I am, over in Quenningwell, come the next elections. And then your uncle'll have to look out for someone else to keep the White House spick and span.'

Susan glanced at Inkpen, who had come out with the bottle of medicine for Elspeth, and she was surprised to intercept an odd glance between them, almost as if they shared secrets. But that was absurd, she thought. Well, anyway, Inkpen had looked as if he were half shaking his head at Alf Dinning to say no more. Perhaps, she thought, if you were only a gardener and putting up for the local Council, it would look better for your chances if you didn't boast about it.

She went back with the medicine, and gave it to Mrs. Boffin to put in some cool place. Thinking of Alf Dinning, she remarked casually, 'I hear my uncle's gardener is putting up for the Council in Quenningwell. Did you know that, Mrs. Boffin?'

Mrs. Boffin, Susan noticed, didn't look at all pleased. 'First of all, miss, there's not much as goes on around here that I don't know, and for another thing, I'm not always pleased by what I hear. You may take that which way you like.'

'Why, Mrs. Boffin, I meant no harm,' Susan said quickly.

'That's all right, miss,' Mrs. Boffin said, as if sorry she had snapped so. 'But you'll find,' she said, hesitating rather, 'that things are not the same here any more. Well, places and people change wherever you go, and after all, it's four years, now, isn't it?'

Susan agreed that it was.

'And there's never a batch of four years to change things so much as the time between a young lady's fourteenth and eighteenth birthdays,' Mrs. Boffin finished firmly. 'I mind me I was eighteen when I married Boffin.' She sounded as if she were on safer ground now and disposed to chat while she made a pot of tea.

'Mr. Boffin was a local man?' Susan enquired delicately. She didn't even know whether he were still alive.

'Was not and is not,' Mrs. Boffin said. 'A seafaring man. Up the creek at Yoxbrook, I met him, one bank holiday. There was me in all my finery — white, it was the custom to wear of a bank holiday in those days — and I'd twisted some wild flowers at my waist and in my hair. It was all hanging down my back, and Boffin always said that I looked ready for anything. Well, we were wed that summer and off he goes to sea and I never saw him since. Still, I had my health and strength and I worked at the vicarage first, until your uncle bought these four cottages and made 'em over. A good man, that uncle of yours,' she finished up.

Susan agreed, but reflected sadly to herself that Mrs. Boffin's life story had served her very well in getting out of discussing with Susan the unexpected turn of events that could probably put her uncle's gardener and odd job man into a seat on the Quenningwell Council.

Susan went up to sit with Elspeth for a while. 'Yoxbrook,' she thought, and pictured it. The creek with the tide out and all that sandy mud that kept imprints of the bare feet in it. They could walk across to the other side, wading through the shallow channel in the middle. And all the gay coloured sail craft would be lying on their sides among the tufts of long grass and weeds, and everything would be still, immobilized, when the tide was out on a summer day in Yoxbrook Creek. She sighed.

'If you want to go to some of the places you used to know, with the others,' Elspeth said suddenly, 'don't mind me. I shall be all right, so long as I can read sometimes.'

'Bless you, you're going to get strong and well and be up and about with the rest of us,' Susan said briskly, and went to pull across one of the long purple curtains, to keep the sun from hitting across Elspeth's eyes.

As she did so, she looked down at the boys, limping home. Frankie was holding a grubby rag half across his face and Colin was half carrying him. Linda, behind them, was angrily telling them something.

Susan said, 'I must go down for a few minutes, pet,' and she hurried out before Elspeth could ask what had happened.

Frankie had a black eye. 'What on earth happened?' Susan demanded.

'It was that boy, that boy, the one hurting the dog, what we saw in the car yesterday, that boy!' Frankie stuttered.

'The silly clot waded in and tried to stop this brute from hurting a cat this time,' Colin said scornfully. 'I told him not to go near the little new houses but you know what he's like. Crusader Frankie, that's him. Help a cat that wouldn't care, and collect a black eye. It's a beauty, isn't it?'

'We're going to have a nice time with you lot, aren't we?' Mrs. Boffin said, her mouth turning down. 'Come to the larder and let me put a nice bit of juicy steak on it. The oldest remedies are best, young man, but don't make me waste too much steak in this house or else you and me are going to fall out!'

That was only the beginning of a very trying day, and it culminated in Susan's having to agree regretfully with Elspeth that the programme she had thought of at first should be started, at least, even without Elspeth, because the children were going to get into trouble if left to their own devices.

Merida floated back in time for lunch and announced that she had discovered a marvellous hair-dressers' in Quenningwell but that she would need a little car.

'But you can't drive yet!' Susan said.

'No, but I know someone who will,' Merida said dreamily.

'Not Lauretta! You're not to send for Lauretta — you know Uncle doesn't approve of her,' Susan said quickly.

'It's a man, dear, and he's so nice.'

'No,' Mrs. Boffin put in unexpectedly. 'A man I cannot and will not allow without your uncle's permission. In charge of you all I am, and you'll take a bus, miss, or ride a bike, I don't mind which way it is, but a strange man in a car I will not allow.'

Susan sighed. Merida and the others were rubbing Mrs. Boffin up the wrong way too quickly. She said to Mrs. Boffin, 'Is there somewhere where I could hire a car to take us for outings, d'you suppose?'

This commended itself to the housekeeper. 'Well, now, there's Tom Lewis — him as is the eldest boy of Oliver Lewis at the farm. Got a corner of Low Meadow, he has, as belongs to his father, and opened up a nice little Service Station. I know for a fact he runs a taxi service. Why don't you go along and have a talk with him, miss? Tell him I sent you.'

Susan decided to do just that. She walked with Merida to the bus stop after lunch. Merida looked happy, a rare occurrence. In London she was too much under her father's control. This was nice here. Freedom, absolute freedom. Susan discussed the hiring of a car with her and Merida said carelessly, 'Do as you like. I'll foot the bill.' She was enjoying having a lot of money to play with and there wasn't a thing her father could do about it because she had inherited it from a relative on her mother's side and there were no strings attached. Lawyers had the bulk in trust for her, but her monthly allowance was dangerously large for someone like Merida.

The boy at the service station couldn't help. He had taxi orders for most of the day and couldn't venture too far because he had only a boy of school-leaving age to help him and to leave at the garage in his absence. Merida waved as the bus went by so Susan was left high and dry with no ideas. What on earth, she thought, could she do with the boys? Walk them?

She found a map of the district in a frame at the cross-roads. This was an innovation and no doubt for the benefit of the new people living in the little new houses on the estate. She stood studying it when a car pulled up behind her and someone gently pipped at her. She turned round to find Gerald Adams.

'Nothing better to do, Susan?' he mocked gently. 'You must know this district like the back of your hand?'

'I've forgotten some of the places,' she confessed, 'and Frankie's made an enemy already and got a black eye, so I thought I'd better hire a car and take them all further afield for some trips but Tom Lewis can't leave the garage for long.'

'I'm going up to the farm. Want to renew your acquaintance with the man you plagued so much not so long ago? We'll talk about it on the way,' so she nodded and got in beside him. It was the same car, big, leather-upholstered, comfortable, nostalgic. She leaned back and sighed. 'I'm glad we came back here,' she murmured.

He didn't say that he was glad, too, she was puzzled to notice. He did say, however, 'Susan, you're eighteen. Are you engaged to be married yet?'

'Of course not,' she laughed. 'Nothing like that!'

'What are you going to do with your life? Don't let them push you into — ' but he didn't finish. He made a lot out of braking sharply to let a mechanical binder back and turn, to get out of a side lane, and when Gerald Adams had the road to himself again, he talked of other things.

At the farm, Susan looked around her with appreciation. It was one of those low rambling houses so typical of this part of the country. The village had electricity, but up here were the type of table lamps that needed to be pumped up. They gave a brilliant light from their opaque white globes. Mrs. Lewis in the evenings sat with one at her elbow, Susan recalled, and made interminable rag rugs and embroidered antimacassars. They were on every chairback now; needlework pictures of gardens with ladies in crinolines; the cushions had them, they were even framed on the walls instead of samplers.

She was busy at the vast kitchen range. She cooked for all the hands as well as her own vast family. 'So you're back, Susan,' she said, by way of greeting.

Dr. Adams had gone straight through

to the meadow. It was an outside accident. 'Those men!' Norah Lewis said impatiently. 'No more sense than children. They cry like children, too. Don't know how to bear a bit of pain. What are you going to do with your life, child?' she suddenly thrust at Susan.

'You're the second person who has said that to me today,' Susan said. 'I don't know. Nursing, perhaps, but certainly something to do with children.' That had come to her suddenly. Thinking about the boys, and Elspeth's lost look in her eyes, and gallant Linda, standing four-square and telling everyone of her hates, to give herself Dutch courage. 'I must be with children.'

'Yes, well, don't go and give your life to other people's children — you want some of your own. Have you no man, then?'

'That's the second time I've been asked that, as well,' Susan marvelled. 'Dr. Adams asked me that.'

Norah Lewis shot a quick measuring look at Susan. 'Yes, well,' she said again.

'I'm not surprised. You're eighteen, aren't you?'

'I've only just left school,' Susan reminded her gently.

'You should have come down last year,' Norah Lewis said unaccountably. 'You're a year late.'

'But the Twinings were at The White House,' Susan pointed out. 'We couldn't turn them out. Uncle had given them a lease, you know.'

'Those Twinings!' Norah Lewis's disgust was evident. 'Goodness knows what they've been up to.'

'Oh, I don't know,' Susan said. 'They've cleaned out the house wonderfully. You should see it!'

'And that's not all they've cleaned out,' Mrs. Lewis said. 'I didn't like 'em the first time I set eyes on 'em. Too smooth, that's what they were. Far too smooth. Townies.'

Dr. Adams came in then. 'Well, we've fixed young Albert up,' he said cheerfully. 'Tell him not to try and take it out of the tractor next time he's in a

49

temper, will you?' And to Susan, he said, 'Shall I give you a lift, Susan? We were to find someone to drive you all on that picnic, weren't we?'

Susan was puzzled at the way Norah Lewis looked from first one and then the other of them, as if she suspected Gerald Adams of proposing some arrangement she wouldn't care for. Susan thought it might possibly be like this with all the older people she had known four years ago — trying to arrange things for her. Young people did tend to get engaged early in the country and Susan supposed the older ones might think she should be engaged, too. They'd have no need to worry about Merida on that score, Susan thought. She always had an escort at the ready. Susan felt a prick of fear when she remembered Merida. Who might she find to take her to the next picture show or dance?

Gerald Adams said as they drove away from the farm, 'Nice to be back, is it? Seeing all the old friends?' and Susan agreed.

Gerald had two more calls to make, and each time he asked about hire cars. One patient was a garage mechanic, the other a retired bus driver who liked to earn a little by taking the occasional passenger in his second-hand car. Neither could help.

'This is ridiculous,' Susan said. 'Never mind, I can telephone into Quenningwell. Thanks a lot, anyway.'

'I'm only working up a good excuse to offer my services,' Gerald said mildly. 'If you could wait for my day off, I could do the job myself, couldn't I? Well, I used to make a good chauffeur, didn't I?'

'The children would love that,' Susan said. 'I've told them so much about the way it used to be. It seems such a life-time ago. I don't know why my uncle didn't let us continue coming down here.'

'Neither do I,' he said. 'Well, about this wonderful day, I'd better leave the grub to Mrs. Boffin, I suppose, although my housekeeper — '

'Oh, no, remember what happened last time when you provided the picnic basket? Mrs. Boffin was so huffy for days afterwards.'

They laughed over the memory. It was like old times . . . and yet not quite. Susan was bothered over the difference. It was as if there was something about him that scared her; some new facet of his personality that hadn't been there before, or perhaps that she hadn't been aware of. She shut her eyes to it, and talked hard about where they could go. 'What about Yoxbrook?'

He didn't like that idea. He stopped smiling and said he thought not. 'Well, you suggest somewhere, then,' Susan said amiably.

'The other side of Holland Green, I think. In the hills. Somewhere fresh. The boys will be able to run wild without anyone getting upset, and young Linda can get rid of some of her hates, climbing.'

So it was arranged. Susan felt a little glow. The Holiday Doctor was going to be all that she had told the children he had been. All and more, she told herself.

Mrs. Boffin wasn't so pleased when she heard about it, however. It was at supper, which they all had round the big table in the kitchen. It was warm, and the air was full of the smell of Mrs. Boffin's baking of that afternoon. Spicy buns and a rich fruit cake, newly-baked bread, and the boiled pudding that was to follow supper. Mrs. Boffin baked with love. She served the meal as if it were her life's work, Susan thought with a smile, watching her. You couldn't ask to help Mrs. Boffin dish up a meal. They had learned that when they had been there before.

Merida sat yawning, and the boys were so hungry they were prepared to snatch at the hunks of bread in the central basket. Linda was quietly pinching them under the table-cloth. Mischief always lurked when they had to wait, hungry. Susan, sitting resting her head in one hand, her elbow on the table in a comfortable way you could never indulge in at Uncle Damien's house, said lazily, to create the necessary diversion while the meal was being served up, 'We tried to get a hire car for our first outing, Mrs. Boffin, but we couldn't. So Dr. Adams helped out.'

Mrs. Boffin was momentarily but not entirely distracted. 'Oh?' she said. 'Well, he knows enough people in the district, I'm sure. If he can't think of someone to drive you, I can't think who can. Who did he settle on, then?'

The boys were now hanging on Susan's answer. Even Linda had stopped her under-the-cloth pinching. Susan said, 'He's going to make it his day off and drive us himself.'

Mrs. Boffin was caught off guard. Her jaw dropped with surprise, and she let the handle of the pot go, so that the potatoes she was serving bounced all over the table.

3

Everyone dived for them and there was a dangerous scramble, but they were all back in the pot at last, and only two broken plates. Mrs. Boffin was cross and bothered and blamed Susan.

'I'm sorry, but I didn't know you'd be so surprised,' Susan stammered. What on earth was the matter with Mrs. Boffin? She had never been like this in the past! 'You don't *mind* him taking us, do you? I'm sure Uncle Damien wouldn't mind.'

'Your uncle doesn't know anything about it,' Mrs. Boffin said. 'The idea, Dr. Adams suggesting such a thing. He can't do that!'

Alf Dinning echoed that, and looked equally indignant.

'Why can't he?' Susan demanded of them both. 'Do you mean to tell me he can't get away from his practice for one little day? Surely there's another doctor in the place who can help out?'

'Did he tell you he could get off for a whole day?' Mrs. Boffin retorted, but it struck Susan that she seemed relieved. 'Well, he'd better think again if that's what he's a mind to do. He'll be called out, you mark my words, and your whole day messed up. Alf, you just find someone to take 'em. We don't want 'em ringing up strangers in Quenning-well. See if Barretts'll do it.'

After supper, Merida drifted into Susan's room to see if any of her things had been left behind. 'Funny, the hoo-ha about dear Dr. Adams, wasn't it?' she said lazily. Elspeth wasn't asleep. She at once wanted to know what it was all about.

Merida, for once, obliged and told her. Because she wanted to go all over it again, Susan suspected.

'Your dear Holiday Doctor wanted to take the lot of us on a picnic on his day off but Mrs. Boffin was outraged, indignant, the lot, at the mere idea! I wonder why?' she mused, prinking at her eye-lashes in the glass. 'Now if our Susan was at all glamorous, I would suspect Mrs. Boffin thought he was planning to leave the rest of us by some lonely stretch of heath and make off with her!'

'Merida!' Susan expostulated, because Elspeth at once looked alarmed at the lurid picture Merida had painted.

'But she's not, are you, love?' Merida said. 'You wouldn't want to be glamorous so I know you won't be offended. Now if it was me — oh, well, perhaps it's because *I* shall be in the party. Let's try the idea out for size by saying I won't be going. I bet he'll manage to cancel the plan.'

'Merida, keep out of this,' Susan said heatedly. Merida had always spoiled plans in the past, and although she had been relatively quiet lately, it looked as if the old streak of lazy malice was still below the surface.

All the same, Merida must have managed to telephone the doctor next morning to say she couldn't go. When he visited Elspeth, he told Susan that he would have to cancel his day off that week. 'But I have managed to find someone to take you all. In fact, I think he'll be good for driving the lot of you around generally. It's old Matthew Nutt's boy, over at the boatyard. He'll be all right.'

Susan nodded, aware that Elspeth was looking at her. Elspeth watched her closely all the time. It was as if the child were pinning her faith in Susan and Susan alone.

'It's very good of you to bother, Dr. Adams,' Susan said formally. 'I'm sure it will work out very well.'

He glanced up quickly at her. 'Yes, well, I would have liked to go very much but I suppose it was a bit of wishful thinking on my part,' and he put the stethoscope back in his ears and listened a long time to Elspeth's chest, so Susan had no further chance of saying any more. When he took it out again, he said in a pleased voice, 'Chest and back quite clear, so all you've got to do, young woman, is to get strong again,' and after that he talked all the way down the stairs about the other children and it seemed to Susan that he avoided her eyes.

Merida was very pleased with herself, after he had gone. 'See what I mean? As soon as I said I couldn't go, there it was — off!' She dabbed a little more lipstick on her rather full young mouth. 'He really is rather sweet, isn't he, and it honestly doesn't matter that he's so hard up, since I've got so much cash, don't you think?'

Matthew Nutt's boy couldn't come until the Thursday, which left two days in which to plan something to amuse the other children. Susan left Mrs. Boffin in charge of Elspeth and took the boys and Linda on the bus to Quenningwell Fair. It was held on the Market Day, Tuesday. The bus was crowded, and Frankie and Linda were very excited. Frankie kept talking about the boy who ill-treated animals. His black eye was fading slowly, and he was inclined to look behind him a lot, nervously, but Susan decided to take no notice of that. They were to have lunch in Quenningwell and come back on the four o'clock bus. Susan felt that that would be quite enough for the first day single-handed, and she wondered how she could persuade Merida to come with her in future. Merida had gone out before breakfast. Too late Susan realized why she had wanted a room of her own; Elspeth's little room had had a long window which none of them had investigated at first. Later it had turned out to be a glass door to the white-painted wooden steps leading down to the garden.

'That girl knew it,' Mrs. Boffin said wrathfully that morning. 'I meant to lock that window and take the key away, but there, thinking young Elspeth was to be there, and her delicate and not likely to be venturesome like the others, I just didn't bother. That Merida, sly, that's what she always was, and always will be.'

Susan didn't say anything about that. It was no use. Mrs. Boffin had always held to her own views, and she wasn't far wrong about Merida. Under that endearing, mischievous smile, there had always lurked something you couldn't quite trust in Merida.

Susan concentrated on the day at the Fair. This wasn't difficult at first because there was so much to see that was interesting; so much to show them that she remembered from the last holiday. The bus went a different way to Quenningwell and instead of the road that Uncle Damien's chauffeur had taken, the bus plunged down hill roads, narrow and (from the children's point of view) exciting; five cows blocked the road at the foot of Windmill Hill, and a tractor got jammed with a car-carrying vehicle that Frankie was almost hysterical with excitement over. There was a great crane on a building site that took his attention, too.

The children stopped talking to Susan and conversed together and she fell into a dream about Gerald Adams, trying to decide what was so different about him. He had a curious intent way of looking at her, which she didn't remember from the past. In those days he had treated her almost like a young sister; casually, with a degree of friendliness that warmed the heart over the years. Now it was almost as if he wanted to slip back into that old casual friendliness and didn't quite dare. It was all very puzzling.

There was an argument going on about mushrooms and toadstools. A woman had some rather battered mushrooms in her shopping basket. It reminded Susan of something she had meant to ask the children earlier.

'Mrs. Boffin said she was pleased the mushrooms had been gathered for breakfast. Who gathered them?' Susan asked.

Ordinarily the person who had done the good deed would be so virtuous as to fall over himself to claim the credit. Susan had discovered that much in the short time she had known them. This time they looked uneasily at each other and no one would own up.

'Now what's the matter?' she demanded.

'Frankie got them,' Linda said.

'Telltale! You got some, too!'

'Never mind, Frankie. It was a kind thought and so long as Mrs. Boffin was satisfied that they *were* mushrooms, then that's all right. When did you get them?'

'He crept out of the kitchen window at five this morning,' Linda blurted out.

Colin pretended to be vastly interested in a motorcyclist who was trying to edge past their bus with inches to spare.

'But you can't do that!' Susan exploded. 'You know that's not right, Frankie! Colin, why did you let him?'

'Colin went with him,' Linda said, enjoying herself now.

Susan had to separate them. 'Now listen, all of you. This is no way to behave on a bus or anywhere in fact. And you are not, repeat not, to go out of the house before Mrs. Boffin is down and it's all opened.'

'Why?' Linda asked, in her forthright way.

'Well,' Susan said helplessly, 'because Mrs. Boffin and I happen to be responsible for you all, and if anything happened to you, how could we help you, if we didn't even know you weren't safely in your beds?'

'We could have a dog,' Colin said thoughtfully.

'Never mind that,' Susan said, refusing to be side-tracked. 'If you don't promise to keep in your rooms until you're called, then I shall have to write and tell Uncle Damien and he'll bring us all back and we shall have to spend the summer holidays at his London house, and I can't think any of you would like that!'

There was a short silence, and then Frankie said, 'But there's things *going on* and we've got to find out what they are!'

Susan thought he meant that things

were going on in the nature world. It was understandable. The country-side had always beckoned to her at that deathly still hour, before the world was up. She said, 'If you're so mad keen to go out at five, give me a call and I'll go with you.' And she didn't understand the look they all exchanged.

I'll tell Dr. Adams about it, she told herself. He'll know what to do. Already he was becoming a prop, the strong man in her life.

Quenningwell looked different today. There were streamers of bunting across the roads, and great banners advertising the Fair. Flags flew from the poles on top of the buildings, and there were banks of flowers massed around the Town Hall. It did coincide with a new building being opened, but the children weren't interested in that. It was the fairground they wanted.

They had never seen a fair. Suddenly Susan brightened up as she realized what an opportunity she had with them. They had never seen anything like this, of course, having lived most of their lives in the Middle East. She decided to let them go on everything. What harm would it do? It wasn't as if Elspeth, the delicate one, who was liable to faint with fright, was there with them.

They pushed through the crowds in the High Street and bought bars of chocolate and they darted into a sixpenny store and spent more of their pocket money on bottles of pop with straws but here was a set-back. They didn't want to leave the counter with the toy guns.

'But at the Fair there'll probably be a shooting range where you can try out the real thing,' Susan protested, and that persuaded them to move on. Susan held on to Linda's hand, under protest, but the boys pushed ahead. They couldn't believe that there would be real guns for the taking. 'What else is there?' they kept coming back to demand.

For Susan the first part of that day

was a happy one. Linda's eyes were literally dancing after she came off the Scenic Railway. She had even forgotten to find someone to hate. Frankie sampled The Mat, but was disgusted to find smaller children than himself on it, so he settled for a thing called The Caterpillar, which went round at a terrific rate, the little train tilting with the turntable, and at the same time a shade kept going over the top, sideways, and folding back again. It looked like a caterpillar, but Susan was very doubtful of what the sensation would be like to be a passenger.

The children dragged her on. 'Oh, come with us! Don't be chicken,' they said. People in the crowd laughed. Suddenly Frankie stopped chattering at top speed and muttered urgently, 'There's that man again! Look, the one from El Shabah!'

They were all looking, over Susan's shoulder, but the crowd behind them was urging them on, towards the turnstile. Susan looked behind but could see no particularly dark face, and then she had to fumble with her purse and the moment was lost.

'You missed him,' Frankie cried in agony. 'He was an Arab and he was wearing a shawl — '

'Striped,' Linda put in, 'and a hair cord round it, but he'd got an ordinary suit on — '

'But he was from El Shabah,' Frankie said. Susan settled them in the train, Linda by her side, Frankie with his brother. Susan nodded to Colin. 'Hold on to him. He's getting excitable again!' she said, but Colin leaned forward and murmured, 'He's right, you know. I saw the chap, too.'

'Well, what if you did see someone from back home? Is there anything to be afraid of?' Susan asked in exasperation.

'He's after us,' Frankie shrilled, but his voice was almost lost in the concerted shriek of the passengers as the Caterpillar moved off.

It was a hideous experience, that

ride, but the children loved it. Susan was sure she must look green when she staggered off. She felt terrible.

'Look, you've been on The Mat, the Scenic Railway, the Water Chute, the Old Dark House and now this thing. It's time for a rest and a cup of tea. Come along. Besides, I want to talk to you all.'

There was a restaurant of sorts. Tables and chairs were set about on the grass under big coloured sunshades. Susan and Colin went and bought cups of tea without any saucers, and fizzy lemonade for Linda and Frankie. Linda slipped away and bought choc ices, but when they were seated and busy with the drink, Susan said, 'Now what about this man from El Shabah? *Is* there such a man, Colin?'

'Yes,' he said coolly.

'Why didn't you tell Uncle Damien about it?' Susan demanded.

'Because he didn't ask me.'

'Well, how could he ask you if he didn't know about such a person? What does the man want, anyway? Is he a servant? Does he know you? Why does Frankie look scared when he thinks he sees him?'

'Because he's going to kidnap me,' Frankie said.

Susan was alarmed, and then common sense made her laugh, shortly it was true, because Frankie really did let his imagination run riot. 'Things don't happen like that in this country,' she said firmly. 'You may have seen such a person, but there are people in Quenningwell and big towns like this, from all over the world. They come here to work, and if they look at you, it probably means that they've just looking at everything and everyone because it's all so new to them.'

'He'll get me,' Frankie said, as if Susan hadn't spoken.

'Me, too,' Linda said ghoulishly.

'It's a lot of rot!' Susan said again, but she wished with all her heart that Dr. Adams were with her just then. Quite apart from her own odd feeling about him and how he had changed, there was still that rocklike quality about him, and he would have settled this matter in no time. 'Come on, if you've all finished, I know just the thing we ought to see next. It's called The Hall of Mirrors — but after that we'll have to go easy because I'm running out of cash. I'd forgotten how expensive all these things are to go on.'

The last time they had gone into the Hall of Mirrors, Susan had been thirteen, and she and Merida had leaned, one on each side, against the Holiday Doctor, laughing so helplessly that it really hurt. And he had taken them — half-carried, half-dragged them? — out to the ice-cream stall and bought them enormous cornets, to cool them down. Today it didn't seem to her quite so funny, although the children laughed inordinately. Did it mean, she asked herself, that the distorted mirrors were only funny the first time, or did it mean that you had to be with someone special to enjoy it? The children dragged her from one to the other of the mirrors and screamed with laughter, without realizing that her own laughter wasn't quite so unrestrained.

And then the laughter of all of them froze. The Arab was behind them again. Frankie shrank back, his face white, his eyes staring. Susan drew herself up, but the man merely bowed and said, 'This little boy is scared of the mirrors, no?'

The children bolted. Susan had never seen them like this before. She half turned to follow them, then turned back, intending to tell the man that he had no right to frighten other people's children like that, but there was no sign of him. He had melted into a crowd who had come in and were holding themselves up laughing at the mirror behind Susan.

She ran out, but now the crowds in the fairground were thicker. There was no sign of the children, or the Arab. Panic seized her. Merida had deserted her that morning, and she ought to have stayed with her. Uncle Damien had said — his last words to them had been — stay together! I don't want to hear of anyone getting lost!

She threshed her way through the crowds, looking first this way and then that. A cold, unnamed fear gripped her middle. It was the most horrible sensation, to be hemmed in by people, strange people, and to know that three children in your care had got lost. How could they have got lost so completely?

Now she was back where she had started, at The Caterpillar. Had they gone on it, she asked herself wildly? She turned back, intending to wait at the turnstile for the next lot to come out, and she ran full tilt into a tall young man in cords and sweater. She clung to him briefly, to get her footing, and she felt his arms round her. She looked up, realization of his identity dawning on her so suddenly, that relief loosened her tongue and she cried in a ringing voice, 'Oh, Dr. Adams, I'm so *glad* to see you!'

He smiled down at her. 'You are, of course, in trouble, Susan!' but he wiped one of her cheeks gently with the back of his hand. It was wet. 'What is it, my dear?'

'I've lost the children,' she said.

'Well, it's nothing to cry about,' and he put one arm round her shoulders and steered her out of that knot of people into a less crowded space. 'Now, I propose to get you a cup of tea, and I'll go in search of them. They're not short of funds, I take it? They'll probably be sampling the things you haven't let them do yet.'

'No, no, you don't understand,' she said wildly.

'Susan, remember where they came from. They haven't seen anything like this before,' he said gently.

'Where they came from — that's exactly it,' she gasped, clinging to his arm. 'You don't understand — there was a man, an Arab. Frankie kept saying he'd seen someone from El Shabah, and then he was there, and the children just bolted. They'd already told me this man was going to kidnap

Frankie. Then the man vanished, and I can't find them.'

'Take it easy, my dear,' he said. 'Frankie's very excitable. There must be a reasonable explanation. You simply must not get all steamed up over those brats. Come on, we'll just take a turn round the show again, just to satisfy you, and then some tea.'

They found the children at last. Both boys were helping Linda along. Her face was dirty and tear-streaked, and there was considerable blood on one of her legs. 'She ran away from that man and caught her leg on some iron,' Frankie shouted excitably.

'All right, take it easy,' Dr. Adams said again. It must have been the fourth time he had said it, and it was already having some effect on Susan. She just wanted to sit down and cry with the relief of the children having been found. 'Let's have a look at that leg.'

It was a nasty place, so he took Linda to the First Aid Station, and dressed it there. Susan tackled the boys. 'What happened? Why did you run away like that?' she asked in sheer exasperation.

'It was a good idea,' Colin said. 'We'd agreed that if we saw that man again, we'd split up. He couldn't chase all three of us in different directions, and the two that got away would come to the rescue of the one that was caught.'

'Colin, that may be adventure to you, but if grown-ups were really chasing you, you couldn't hope to do much. Don't you see? The best thing is to stay with me. I would have appealed to the crowd to help us.'

'This crowd's no help,' Colin said. 'We tried that and they just stared, and there were more chaps with him — '

'Now don't tell me you had a lot of Arabs chasing you. Oh, no, you're just making it up.'

Frankie danced about. 'He isn't, he isn't, they're going to kill us.'

She smiled. Suddenly it wasn't so awful because Gerald Adams was with them. He would be back with Linda soon, and everything would be smoothed out. She said, 'What would they be doing that for?'

'Because of what we know about them,' Colin said. He talked with such a calm practical air that it was most convincing. Susan couldn't repress a shudder. Suppose there was any truth in it? After all, they had lived in the Middle East, and if they had got into as much mischief there as they were already getting into here, it might not be so funny!

Suddenly it was all explained. Susan caught sight of a sideshow with minarets and mosques painted up all round it, and the words: The Great Ali from El Kitrouh and his Lovely Dancing Ladies. Two Arabs stood trying to entice the crowd to buy tickets and go in.

'Oh, boys, how could you frighten me so?' Susan cried. 'Look — that's where your Arabs came from, and I doubt if they're real Arabs at that!' and just then Dr. Adams came along with Linda, her knee heavily bandaged and a most convincing limp to that leg.

'Let that be a lesson,' Gerald Adams grinned at Susan. 'Don't take too much notice of what these scamps tell you. I've already heard another tall story from this young lady.'

'But it's true,' Linda protested. 'There are mysterious goings on in the village — Frankie will tell you. He heard — '

Frankie glared at her and Colin said, 'Shut up!' Gerald Adams laughed. 'Everyone all right now? Then I suggest some lunch and I'm the man to provide it. Come on, everyone.'

Over lunch, he said to them, 'I remember a good many tall yarns I told my family at your age, but I made them convincing!'

'How did you come to be here?' Susan thought to ask him. The nightmare of having lost the children, had tended to make his appearance so acceptable that she hadn't questioned it at the time. Now she thought it rather odd.

'I called to see Elspeth. She told me where you'd all gone, and that Merida wasn't with you. I just had to satisfy myself that you were managing all right single-handed. Good thing, wasn't it?' And again he directed that odd searching look at her. 'Why wasn't Merida with you, Susan?'

She shifted uneasily. 'I didn't even know she'd gone out, but she wouldn't have been much help. Better if she's found something to interest her. After all, she *is* seventeen.'

'You're trying too hard,' he murmured. 'I sense that you are seething inside, because she escaped.'

Susan smiled ruefully. 'Uncle Damien wouldn't like it if he knew. Don't tell him, will you?'

'Will I have the chance?'

She frowned. 'You know what Uncle Damien's like. He might just take it into his head to telephone you, or even to pay a flying visit and ask you what had been going on.'

'Then I won't say a word — provided you all back me up by being very well behaved,' he said severely to the children. 'Does anyone care for roller skating? There's a very good rink in the town.'

That was a tremendously popular suggestion, and one that worked out well for Susan, who could sit and watch the children having fun without fear of losing them.

'If you want to continue your rounds or anything,' she said to Dr. Adams. 'you get off. I'm most grateful to you for turning up when you did, and everything, but I wouldn't like to feel — I mean I don't want to — '

As she broke off in confusion, he said, 'You mean you don't especially want me to stay?'

She looked away. 'No, I didn't mean that, but I know how busy you are, and when we told Mrs. Boffin that you'd offered to drive us for a whole day, she was very cross with us.'

'Was she!' He stopped smiling, and frowned at the roller skaters. 'Did she say just why she was cross?'

'I gathered that she thought we were

taking a mean advantage of an old friendship and that you didn't like to refuse us.'

'I assure you, Susan, it was no such thing,' he said quietly, and his tone was so convincing that she accepted it and relaxed.

She felt wonderful with him. It was a kind of happiness she had never had before. It felt as if she had known him all her life. It didn't matter any more what Mrs. Boffin thought or anyone else. At that moment Susan was at one with him; she belonged to him.

They sat watching the children, not talking now. It didn't matter what Merida was doing, either, or that Uncle Damien, if he did take it into his head to come down, would assuredly find fault with her, automatically. She was in a kind of special place, with Gerald Adams, and her face reflected the deep tranquillity she was feeling. He looked at her and smiled, and looked away again.

It was the shortest afternoon Susan had ever known. It seemed unfair that it should slide away so quickly, as if Fate were snatching brief happiness from her. Gerald Adams decided that they had all better be making a move. He remembered a call he had promised to make on an outlying patient; not an urgent case, but he must get there just the same.

'Let me know how Linda's leg is,' he said to Susan.

She smiled broadly. 'There doesn't seem much wrong with it.'

'Ah, you never know,' he said, and they both laughed.

For some reason best known to herself, Susan didn't tell Mrs. Boffin about the special part of the day that concerned Dr. Adams. She made up her mind not to mention it when she noticed how the children neatly side-stepped the subject. Susan listened to them in amazement, rattling away at Mrs. Boffin, telling her about the Arab who had chased them, and about every single thing they had done by way of entertainment, but not a single word about Gerald Adams.

Even when Mrs. Boffin commented: 'I see you've had your leg done up properly — what happened, then, and who did it?' Linda didn't mention Gerald Adams. She said, in a rather surly voice, 'You may not have heard of it, Mrs. Boffin, but there's a First Aid Post at the Fair with a bossy woman in charge who doesn't like children,' and that made Mrs. Boffin laugh and she didn't ask any more about the leg.

Susan felt conscience-stricken. When she had the children alone, she said to them, 'Why didn't you mention Dr. Adams to Mrs. Boffin?'

She was getting used to their innocent regard now, when asked an awkward question. 'She didn't ask us,' they said in unison.

It really was too trying, that answer, and weakly Susan let the point go because she, too, didn't want to talk about him. She didn't want Mrs. Boffin to say something like: 'Really, he should have known better!' because why should he have known better? He enjoyed it, didn't he? She thought of him, sitting relaxed and happy beside her at the roller skating rink. If that wasn't happiness on a man's face, Susan didn't know what it was.

Merida wasn't anxious to disclose what she had been doing, either, but she looked very pleased with herself, and she had bought some new clothes: fine cashmere jerseys with polo collars, filmy underwear, high-heeled shoes. 'The shops aren't half bad in Quenningwell,' she said, and she looked at Susan. Susan was sure that she had seen her and Dr. Adams together in Quenningwell, but she dare not say so.

Susan had other problems, anyway. Frankie got tangled with the boy who had been ill-treating the dog. It was odd, really, the way that flared up. It was a thing that Susan could discuss with Mrs. Boffin and she did. With Alf Dinning, too.

'I'm very worried about it, Mrs. Boffin. I mean, we were nuisances, but we were girls, and we didn't work up fights with anyone, but Frankie's been spoiling for a fight with that boy ever since he came here. Just because he saw him ill-treating a dog.'

'And got a juicy black eye over it,' Mrs. Boffin said with what seemed to Susan like satisfaction.

'It isn't over yet,' Susan said anxiously. 'I'm sure I ought to stop it. He's even found out the boy's name — it's Dickie Stogden.'

'I'd leave them alone, if I were you, Miss Susan.'

Alf Dinning added to that, 'Make a man of him. Looks a little weakling to me!'

'He is not!' Susan was most indignant. 'He may have a thin body and a white face but he's very brave and he won't be beaten.'

'Those Stogdens are not your sort, Miss Susan,' Mrs. Boffin said. 'How would it be if you took the boys for a nice long walk?'

'What, at five in the morning? That's when Frankie goes out to fight Dickie

Stogden. He's supposed to be picking mushrooms but I know better.'

'Well, I tell you this, Miss Susan, what ever he does, *if* he goes out at five o'clock in the morning, it isn't to tangle with any of the Stogden brood, because I happen to know for a fact that none of them are early risers.'

That comforted Susan a little, until the following morning when something woke her and she saw by the illumined hands of her clock that it was only five. The sun wasn't above the horizon and all the world outside her window shimmered with pre-dawn light. Pearly, translucent, with a wine-sharp nip in the air that enchanted Susan. And then she saw Frankie going out with Colin just behind him. Colin couldn't be quiet to save his life. He dropped his gum boots with a double thud that in turn knocked the lid off the dustbin. Someone's dog started to bark, and both boys abandoned their attempt at trying to be quiet and fled.

Susan was in a quandary. Already

Elspeth had awakened in the other bed and was asking anxiously what was happening.

'Mrs. Boffin will happen soon if things don't quieten down,' Susan said grimly. 'She never did like dogs barking at this hour,' and she told Elspeth the time and tucked her down again.

'Are you going out after them?' Elspeth's clear little voice said, a few minutes later.

'After who?' Susan said softly.

'Frankie and Colin,' Elspeth said collectedly. 'I heard them talking about it. The bunks are just behind this wall at my head. When it's quiet their voices come through.'

'Well, in that case, young lady, hadn't you better tell me just what is going on? I had a terrible time in Quenningwell at the Fair because they said an Arab was chasing them but it turned out to be one of the men in a pretend Arab side-show with Arab dancing girls and that sort of thing. So I don't want any old fairy story this time.'

Elspeth thought about that. 'They think there's something going on in the village,' she said at last.

'I know that much, my dear. They told me that. But they wouldn't say what!'

Elspeth said, 'It's a secret. Among the grown-ups. Frankie and Colin don't know what it is. They've gone to find out.'

Susan was frankly alarmed. 'Now listen — all right, pet, I'm not cross with you. But do try and think of everything you've heard them say, because it could be important. Don't you see — we don't live here. We're only visitors. If — *if* the people who live here have got a secret, it isn't for visitors to find out, least of all the children of the visitors. That isn't at all the thing, don't you see?'

For once, the amenable Elspeth didn't see. 'It's only adventure, Susan, and if grown-up people don't want children to have adventures finding out, then they really shouldn't talk about their secrets out in the open air where anyone can overhear, should they?'

'Who talked about their secrets?' Susan demanded, and for no good reason she thought of Inkpen the chemist, who had always struck her as being sinister. If a man like a chemist, who is in the public eye all the time, chooses to move about furtively, then he must surely expect people to wonder why! But on the heels of that thought came the recollection of many sinister-looking people near where they lived, who had excited Susan's imagination as a child, and later she had discovered that it was merely a freak of nature and the people concerned just couldn't help being like that.

Elspeth said, 'You're going to be cross with Frankie and Colin if I tell you, aren't you?' but at last she admitted, 'Well, there was this man — '

'Which man, pet? Try and be more explicit.'

'I don't think I know what that word means and anyway, how can I be anything? I haven't been out of here since we arrived because I'm not well, and I only know what Frankie and Colin were talking about.'

'I'm sorry, pet. I shouldn't have jumped on you, but it is rather worrying because I don't know what they're up to.'

'There was this man and he was behind a wall and he said something like, 'It's to happen tonight' so Frankie and Colin were going to see what was going to happen.'

'Where were they going to see, and where was this wall?' Susan asked. 'Oh, Elspeth, try, darling, try to be very careful and only say exactly what they said.'

'I am trying, but Mrs. Boffin called them down to supper so I didn't hear any more,' Elspeth said. 'Have I been a help?'

'Yes! Oh, yes, you have!' Susan said, because Elspeth was so anxious, and looked near to tears of disappointment. But to herself she said softly, 'Oh, my goodness, what am I to do? Is there really a secret, and is there danger in it for the children? If only I knew where they'd gone!'

Elspeth said unexpectedly, 'Don't worry, Frankie's form master told him once that he wouldn't be a Man until he'd had half a dozen black eyes and Frankie says he's going to be brave enough to get them, so even if he doesn't find out what the secret is, he will be doing something useful, won't he?'

Susan found there was a lump in her throat, as she tried to answer. 'Yes, darling, he really will be doing something useful in that case.'

'And Colin's a very decent elder brother because he doesn't pamper Frankie. He keeps telling him to shut up, for his own good. He told me so.' And Susan said yes, she was sure that was so.

It was strange, the different way they all looked at it. Mrs. Boffin was inclined to be amused, but whether that was at the boys' mischief or Susan's anxiety over them, Susan couldn't decide.

Merida, on the other hand, was inclined to believe the boys. 'My friend says there are always goings-on in villages,' she said with a little flutter and wriggle of the shoulders which made Susan turn sharply on her.

'What friend? Merida, you haven't been scraping acquaintances?'

'Don't be silly,' Merida said airily. 'Peregrine is a very nice man and he knows all the best people.'

Susan felt the ground was being cut from under her feet by the way her family was behaving. 'Peregrine who? How did you meet him? Merida, what will Uncle Damien say?'

'My father won't say anything if no one goes and tells him, and Peregrine Jotham was introduced to me so he's all right. If you want to know, he's actually Lauretta's friend.' She said that rather nervously, waiting for the explosion from Susan, and it came.

'Lauretta! Merida, you didn't ask her to come down here? Well, she can't stay here this time — you know that. There isn't room and anyway Uncle Damien said you weren't to — '

'Oh, Sue, dry up,' Merida begged. 'She's staying in Quenningwell at one of the hotels, and she came down under her own steam — well, yes, she did come to see me, but also to see her friend Peregrine who happened to be staying with relatives in the neighbourhood. Well, why not? There's good fishing and sailing in the district, in case you've forgotten while you've been baby-sitting.'

Susan held on to her temper. This was the way a row started and Susan didn't want that. Not with all the other nagging anxieties she had with the children.

Merida said quickly, 'Anyway, Peregrine knows your Holiday Doctor, so that makes him all right, surely? Actually he's a patient — well, dear Dr. Adams stitched Peregrine's finger up when he cut it on a tin last time they took the boat out.'

Susan decided that that made it a

little better because now she could ask Gerald Adams what this Jotham man was really like. But Lauretta was another matter. 'Merida, you really ought not to see Lauretta, you know. Your father doesn't approve of her.'

'Are you suggesting I should cut her dead if she speaks to me in the street?' Merida protested, looking injured. 'Besides, she got a new car and she's going to take me around, and we have no transport ourselves and you won't let me buy one. I'd love to buy a car. I know just the sort — '

'There's a question of insurance and driving licence and all that sort of thing,' Susan said mechanically, thinking then of Frankie and Colin and of what they had discovered. Other people's secrets . . . why couldn't those boys mind their own business?

It was much later in the day when Frankie and Colin came back. 'Look at those two!' Mrs. Boffin exclaimed standing at the window. She was chuckling, in unwilling admiration, Susan was shocked to discover. 'I wonder how many they took on in the neighbourhood to get knocked about like that! Wonder who won? Well, they did, by the looks of them! Talk about cock o' the walk — just look at that skinny little lad Frankie!' She went to the door and called to them.

The boys were really in a dreadful state but both were jubilant. Frankie said, 'That Dickie Stogden brought his big brother Reg and we licked 'em, me and Colin,' he said at top speed and with a fine disregard for grammar. 'We licked 'em, didn't we, Colin? And now we're friends — me and Dickie and Colin and Reg, we're friends. And the ole Holiday Doctor's coming over in a minute to give us the once over in case we've broken any bones. Well, that's what he said.'

'Why did you have to go and bother him?' Susan said wrathfully.

'We didn't. He saw us. He was walking along and he saw us and he made us tell him where we'd been and he laughed, didn't he, Colin?'

Colin was nodding, and meantime making inroads in a slab of cake he had helped himself to, at the dresser; Mrs. Boffin's new cake that was cooling. And she didn't scold him for interfering with it. She had something else on her mind.

'That Dr. Adams! It doesn't take much to send him haring over here every five minutes,' she muttered, slewing round to glare at Susan as if it were her fault.

Merida said, 'Oh, that's all right. It's because I said I couldn't go out for the day and he cancelled it. I expect he'll want to fix up something else.' She examined her false eyelashes closely in the mirror over the sink, but Mrs. Boffin continued to stare almost accusingly at Susan.

4

Five days they had been there, and
already nothing but trouble, Susan
reflected, as she left Elspeth with plenty
of reading matter, a jug of cold fruit
juice and a glass to hand, and a little
bell she could tinkle if she wanted
something. Five days, and already Dr.
Adams had been in and out, and
everyone said he was so busy! The glow
of happiness she had when she was with
him, soon became clouded when other
people heard of his presence. Somehow
the thought of him being with Susan
and the children caused a lot of
otherwise nice people to look put out.
She just couldn't understand it. It
wasn't as if she personally sent for him
for every little thing; he either came
because he wanted to, or because he
was accidentally in their vicinity, and
never, Susan reflected, was there a time

when she wasn't thoroughly glad of his help and his strength and comfort.

Again she had to go to Inkpen's, for tablets for Elspeth, and this time she decided, as she wasn't in all that much of a hurry, to go along to Mrs. Kimpster, to renew her acquaintance with the keeper of that fascinating general store. So far, Colin had been the one to do the shopping there, at Mrs. Boffin's firm instigation.

Inkpen was very vague this morning, and asked Susan to come back in half an hour for the prescription, so she went to Mrs. Kimpster's with anticipation. Everything and everyone had changed, according to Mrs. Boffin. Well, now Susan would see for herself so far as Mrs. Kimpster was concerned, at least.

One glance told her how true it was, however. Mrs. Kimpster was far less fat than she had been, for a start, Susan noted, and with the loss of all that shaking plumpness had gone, too, a lot of the jollity. At first Mrs. Kimpster didn't even recognize Susan. Her eyes were bad. She said she was soon going to have glasses.

'So you're Susan, eh? Took your time to come and see me, didn't you, but I expect it's because you're quite the young lady now. Some people will be noticing that too, I reckon. Seen the doctor since you arrived?'

Thinking mainly about Elspeth, Susan said, 'Yes, well, that's really why I haven't been before, Mrs. Kimpster. Colin's been doing the shopping because I've been looking after one of his cousins who's been ill. Dr. Adams has been in and out of our place quite a lot.'

'So I've heard,' Mrs. Kimpster said.

Susan stared unseeingly at the packets of siedlitz powder, the little boxes of flypapers, the bootlaces and sink scrubbers and boxes of can-openers. Even Mrs. Kimpster had changed. She wasn't laughing any more, but then perhaps Susan herself wasn't funny. In the old days her school hat had always been over one ear and her plaits sticking out.

Now her brown hair was worn in a loose knot high on the back of her head; easy to do, easy to keep tidy, and much, much easier on the purse than the constant trips to the hairdresser that were such a feature of Merida's existence.

'How do you find the place, then?' Mrs. Kimpster said, as Susan asked for a yard of elastic and she started with great deliberation to measure it off. 'See a lot of changes, I've no doubt!'

'Well, yes, everywhere,' Susan agreed. 'All those little new houses, and the little bus into Quenningwell has gone! The double-decker ones are so ordinary, just like everywhere else!'

'That's right,' Mrs. Kimpster remarked, 'but it makes for business, all those new families. The kids come in here on the way to the bus for school. Been to Yoxbrook Manor yet?' She grinned as she said it. Their sorties in that direction four years ago hadn't been such a dark secret, it appeared.

'No, when the delicate one is better I'll take all the children there,' Susan said, paying for the elastic.

'I don't think you will,' Mrs. Kimpster said unaccountably.

'Oh, it's all right, the children can walk. I might even take them before Elspeth is well. Come to think of it, I don't think that one would enjoy such a trip much.'

'No, and I reckon I know some other people who won't enjoy you lot going to Yoxbrook Manor,' Mrs. Kimpster said, laughing again. 'That Miss Travers, for a start!'

'Who's Miss Travers?'

'Haven't they told you? I thought not! You'll have to know sooner or later, won't you? In Paris she is just now, shopping, they say, though why she can't go shopping in Quenningwell like the rest of us, I can't think. And when she comes back, you'd best warn those boys of yours to keep off the roads. Her driving — you'd think she owned the roads and no one else was supposed to use 'em. Aston Martin car, she's got. She rips through this village fit to kill half the chickens and she has, too, in the past. But even fowls get a bit of sense in the end. Rush out of the way squawking, they do, when they hear her a mile away.'

'Thanks for the warning,' Susan said. 'But what's she got to do with us going to Yoxbrook Manor?'

'Never heard of Colonel Travers, then?' Mrs. Kimpster asked, leaning on her cash register, a thing she had always said in the past that she would never have.

'Oh, him! The owner! Oh, is he related to her? Don't say they've opened the place up again? Oh, no, they couldn't — it was such a dirty old place. It needed rebuilding almost.'

'That's as maybe. Living in one wing they are! He being her father! So I wouldn't be too keen on trespassing, if I was you, miss. Well, as regards Miss Travers, that's the first thing. In the second place — '

But she never got as far as the second place because a customer came in, so Susan took the opportunity of sliding out. She wasn't sure that she liked Mrs. Kimpster any more and it made her very sad. Had the woman changed so much, or was it simply that Susan herself had grown up? Nothing, she thought with regret, was the same. Not even the Holiday Doctor really. In her heart she still felt he would have been nicer if he had stayed just as she had remembered him.

Still, Susan was glad of the warning about Yoxbrook Manor and decided to postpone that. There would be plenty of time. They still had eight full weeks in which to do that.

Dr. Adams hadn't stayed long this morning, and she had had no chance of talking alone with him about this Peregrine person with whom Merida was friendly. It would have to wait, but Susan was anxious about it.

Merida was preparing to go out when she got back with the tablets for Elspeth. 'Where are you going now?' Susan gasped.

'Out for the day. I shall probably go

out every day, because if I stay here, dear Mrs. Boffin will find me a job in the kitchen, and I don't intend to start any such thing.'

'It's a good chance to learn, isn't it?' Susan objected.

'What would I want to know things like that for, with all my money?' Merida asked reasonably. 'And speaking of my money, you can't say I'm a bad sort in every respect, because I've bought some things to help you keep the kids occupied.' She went into her own room, and came back with a flat, heavy package. 'He wanted this specially — Frankie, that is.'

'What is it?' Susan asked blankly.

'A tape recorder, and a supply of tapes,' Merida said carelessly.

Susan gasped. Elspeth said, 'It looks very expensive.'

'It did cost a bit,' Merida said carelessly.

'But he's only eight! A toy would have done just as well and been much less expensive!' Susan gasped.

'What's money?' Merida shrugged. 'Anyway, he did want it.'

'But Merida, Uncle Damien — '

'It's got nothing to do with my father,' Merida said. 'And if you're worried about expense, you should just see the bill for the cine camera I bought for Colin!'

'Now listen, Merida, I know you're generous to a fault, my dear, but Frankie and Colin are only eight and ten — '

'But they're bright as buttons, so don't tell me they won't know how to work the things. They will. And I've bought a transistor for Linda, so she can wander around with it on at full blast and annoy the village!'

That, of course, would amuse Merida! 'I wish you hadn't,' Susan said.

'Oh, poor brats, leave them alone! It will keep them busy and you'll benefit in the long run. Now what about this cherub here — what do you want?' Merida asked running her finger-tip down the side of Elspeth's pale face. 'How about a super make-up box that you can play with in bed? Well, you've got to learn to make up sooner or later, pet, haven't you? Don't leave it as long as Susan has, or you'll lose the urge and that would be tragic.'

'Why would it be?' Elspeth asked anxiously.

'Because no man will want you, darling. Oh, Sue says she doesn't care if no man wants her, but everyone ought to have a man. You make sure you get one early. There's nothing else a girl ought to want, once she gets into her teens.'

'Merida, don't! It's very bad advice,' Susan urged, with scarlet cheeks and mortified eyes.

Merida laughed, and said she'd try out some eye shadow on Elspeth for fun. She wandered out of the room, humming a gay song. Her heels were very high, and her shoes more straps than anything else. There was a touch of the Continental fashions about the way she dressed. No one else in the village wore a summer frock that had no back at all. Susan couldn't help feeling worried.

In Merida's brief absence, Elspeth took the opportunity to say to Susan, 'She can't give me what I want.'

'What *do* you want, pet?' Susan really wanted to know.

'I want a father.'

This was the sort of remark that Susan dreaded. Elspeth's eyes were enormous and she looked as if she were hiding some deep inner grief. The rest of the family could say as much as they liked, that Elspeth had taken her orphanhood better than the others, but it wasn't true, it just wasn't true.

'I mean someone like Dr. Adams,' Elspeth elaborated. 'I've thought about it. He's young for a father of someone my age, I know, but he's old in his mind. Had you noticed?'

'Yes, I know what you mean,' Susan said softly.

'And it would be absolutely perfect if he married you and you could be my mother,' Elspeth went on.

Susan was alarmed. 'Now listen, pet, I really would much rather you didn't say things like that. I know it's all right, but someone might hear you and if it got about, it might be rather awful. Dr. Adams might be very embarrassed.'

'Oh, no, he wouldn't,' Elspeth said earnestly. 'Because I've spoken to him about it.'

'Oh, Elspeth, you never did! How could you?' Susan cried.

'It's all right. He quite understands. I told him he was my favourite man and that you were my favourite woman and he said I'd made a very good choice and that he liked you an awful lot, too.'

Susan's face cleared. Dr. Adams was very kind and understanding and he had no doubt been pandering to a little child who was far from well. 'Yes, well, I do see, darling, but I think you shouldn't discuss it with him any more.'

And then she looked up and saw Merida standing in the doorway, leaning, as if she had been there for some time. Merida didn't look too pleased.

'Don't bother her with make-up now, Merida,' Susan said quickly, thinking Merida had been hating being kept waiting while Elspeth had been talking.

'I wasn't going to, actually,' Merida drawled, her generous mood gone for the time being. 'I was just going to say that now I've bought a little time for you, by giving the kids complicated presents, perhaps you won't be so eager to try and restrict my movements. After all, I'm only going out with Lauretta today.'

'And her friend Peregrine?' Susan breathed.

'Maybe, but it's doubtful,' Merida shrugged, and went out. Susan watched her go down the path, a new cashmere cardigan the exact shade of the silk of her dress, swinging in one hand. She was so much the product of the town. The boy on the milk cart gave her a wolf whistle and she smiled at him, that adorable smile that wasn't quite so blatant as a come-hither smile and yet it wasn't entirely innocent of invitation.

Susan, watching her, was frankly worried. She was only a year older herself, but Uncle Damien, in his usual hectoring, unreasonable way, had put her in charge of all of them.

'Don't worry,' Elspeth said from behind her. 'Nothing will happen to Merida.'

'What makes you say that? I wasn't worrying about her,' Susan lied, for the child's sake.

'Yes, you were. I can tell when you're worrying about someone. There's a special sort of look about your back. I can't explain it. It's as if you're all screwed up inside and it shows on your back. You shouldn't worry about Merida, really you shouldn't. I read in a book yesterday that nothing happens to people like her because she's too selfish to do anything risky.'

'Oh dear, the stuff you get hold of to read,' Susan said, going over to the child and giving her a hug. 'What am I going to do with you?'

'Stay with me, for ever and ever,' Elspeth said. 'There's no one like you.

Dr. Adams says so, so it must be true! It's not just me saying it, you see!'

Susan rather wished that Dr. Adams wouldn't agree with everything that Elspeth said. Other people might misconstrue. Though how did it matter, really? He was free to say what he liked about anyone, wasn't he? And yet there was that sensation of a heaviness in the air, almost as if everyone felt that by being their doctor, he had to be rather — what? Behind a wall, not thinking as other men did? Not free to look at Susan with that intent look of his, nor free to drive her about and talk with her when he came over to visit Elspeth?

She put the incomprehensible thought away while she struggled with other things. The search for the children, to get them ready for when Matthew Nutt's boy came with the car, because this was the day he had settled to take them into the hills; a long way that was too far for Linda to walk, and too much out of the way for local buses to be used.

Matthew Nutt's 'boy' turned out to

be a man with a lean face, something of his father's brows and deep-set suspicious eyes, and also his father's silence. He drove them to the hills, left them there to go on to a job for his father and another job he had to do for himself, and then to return to the cross-roads to pick them up in time to come home to tea.

Susan went with misgivings, but it turned out to be a rather pleasant day. They were far enough away from Holland Green to avoid any of the people they knew, and the children had uninhibited fun together. They didn't know about Merida's gifts yet, and Susan had said nothing. It was a nice day, with no problems. It was true that Frankie did his top-speed boasting about having licked Dickie Stogden, and been invited by his brother time and time again to shut up, and Linda still had a few 'hates', it appeared, but on the whole it was peaceful.

Frankie had brought a lot of jars and boxes with him, in a great cardboard box which hadn't pleased Matthew Nutt's son very much, nor would it if he found out that Frankie had his specimens in it. Frankie mobilized the other two to collect a lot of crawly things for him and Linda wanted some so they shared them out. 'I never knew so many nasty things were out in the woods,' Susan shuddered.

'There's a nature study book I'd like to buy with my pocket money,' Frankie stuttered, trying to count out his six-pences and at the same time hang on to a particularly repulsive centipede sort of animal. 'Could we go into Quenning-well and get it, Sue? There's no bookshop in daft old Holland Green!'

Susan was overcome with delight at the thought of Frankie actually wanting to buy a book and put in some serious reading.

'I'll treat you to it, if you tell me what it's called and who publishes it,' she said, smiling. 'It's all right! I'm going into Quenningwell to get some books for Elspeth, too.'

'Can I come too?' he shrilled.

'You'd better all come, so I know where you are and what you're doing. I wish you wouldn't be so nosey about other people's business. It really isn't nice, you know!'

'How did you know?' Colin asked coldly.

'I saw you both slipping out at five one morning.'

'Yes, well, that's only nature walks,' Frankie said quickly, 'and that reminds me — Sue, would you let us go into Willenfield Woods? It's super in there. Dickie Stogden told us so. He goes in there a lot. He says it's super.'

'Now just a minute, young man. First of all, why are you asking me all of a sudden — you never do! You usually please yourself where you go!'

They all looked rather guilty, but Frankie recovered and said quickly, 'I thought it would be good manners on account of you being decent and offering to treat me to that book I want.'

That totally disarmed her, so she abandoned that point and tackled another and far more important point. 'Why are you friendly with that Stogden boy after you kept fighting him? You hated him at first!'

'Yes, but I licked him, so that's different,' Frankie said, with an air of having explained everything.

'But the fact that you won the fight doesn't change anything, Frankie! He's still a boy who ill-treats animals. You said so yourself. That was the first thing you noticed about him when we were arriving by car — you said he was ill-treating a little dog.'

'No, it was a big dog, and he wasn't ill-treating it. We found out since that he was tangling with it, trying to get a bone out of its throat only it wouldn't let him, because dogs don't know any better when you're trying to help them and it hurts.'

'Oh, so there was really no need to fight him at all!'

'Yes, there was,' Frankie said patiently.

'He's lived here a long time and I've only just come, so I had to fight him so's he'd know I was all right. Same like with my brother Colin.'

His grammar didn't improve and he got more persuasive every day, Susan thought helplessly. She glanced at the other two for support, but they were both behaving as if they were deaf and so knew nothing of what had been said.

She sighed. Again she felt herself wishing uncontrollably that Gerald Adams were here. He would know how to handle this. He could handle boys so well.

Frankie said, 'Well, can we go into Willenfield Woods?'

'I suppose so,' she said, 'but what about that cat you said the Stogden boy was hurting? You can't talk your way out of that!'

'It was lost and he was trying to grab hold of it to take it to old Miss Sims because he thought it was her cat but it wasn't.' That much off his chest, Frankie pushed his own problem further. 'Dickie Stogden goes to a super school and his parents don't have to pay anything. It's all free and they teach him super things, not like the rotten old school we went to.'

Susan winced. She had heard all about the very expensive schools these children had attended. She said, 'I hardly think Uncle Damien will settle for you going to the school the Stogden boy goes to.'

'It'll save him money,' Frankie offered hopefully. 'And they teach Dickie how to make a 'hide' with branches and twigs like a wigwam and you can wriggle inside it and watch the animals and birds mating — '

'Do they! If I hear another word about all this, I shall get on the telephone to Uncle Damien, right away!' Susan threatened.

Frankie, with great common sense, let the argument slide, and the rest of the day passed peacefully. So peacefully, in fact, that Susan forgot about it, rather unwisely.

The weather was wonderful. Slumbrous heat bathed the still countryside, and rose in waves from the pavements in Holland Green. The boys and Linda loved it, and Merida showed them a very glamorous swimsuit and flower-trimmed swim cap she had bought, for the purposes of the circular pool in a roadhouse that Lauretta and her man-friend had discovered, an hour's drive away. But Elspeth suffered under the heat, and inevitably Gerald Adams was calling at the house again.

After his visit was over, he took Susan aside. 'How are the children getting on?' he asked.

'Fine. Why?' She frowned because there was something in his manner that she didn't understand.

'I suppose you can't watch them all the time, but I hear talk about them. People are saying they've been in Willenfield Woods.'

'That's very likely. I've said I don't mind in the daytime but I did rather draw the line at bird-watching in the dark, which was what they wanted to do.'

'But didn't you know that the woods have been enclosed, Susan?' he asked in some surprise.

'Enclosed? Our woods?' She was so indignant.

Dr. Adams laughed at her expression. 'Oh, Susan, my dear, they never were anyone's woods but the owners'!'

'But they were never marked private,' Susan said in dismay. 'Oh, I've told them so much about going into those woods, and taking that old boat out on the lake — I know they belonged to the owner of Willenfield House but no one ever said anything — I mean, everyone went into those woods — '

'I know,' he agreed. 'But the old man died, in those four years you were away, and the new owner has put fences all round, and Trespass notices.'

'Those four years!' she said wrathfully. 'Everything's happened in those four years to spoil everything. Everything's changed, so has everybody. Even you!' She hadn't meant to say it, but it slipped out. She eyed him with some temerity because he looked so stern, and he seemed so much older than she was all of a sudden. Much, much older than he had been before, though she had always known he was very much her senior. As she stood there she tried to work out how old he could possibly be. Twelve, fourteen years older than she was? At this time it seemed a lifetime older than she was, so that he could never understand the queer lost feeling that kept invading her.

'I know, my dear,' he said gently. 'I know. But don't feel too bad about it. It's a matter of adjusting. You'll do it, I know you will. Meantime, Robert Hibbs, who owns Willenfield House, isn't such a bad chap. If you like, I'll speak to him about the children. He might make a concession on their behalf — '

'We don't want any concessions,' she said angrily. 'I'll tell the children to keep away from the beastly woods. After all, there are plenty of other places. Yox-brook, for instance,' she began, and then broke off, bleakly remembering that that, too, had been taken over. 'No, I forgot, someone's taken that, too. Well, surely the Creek is still free?'

He nodded, smiling. 'You were such a little rebel. You never stopped to ask if those places you went to were private, but they were, you know, even then. You trespassed, with the rest of them, and you never turned a hair. Now you're being all outraged because the owners have decided to call halt. Aren't you?' and he touched her chin. It was just a casual touch, an uncle-ish touch, really, but it sent sparks fanning outwards all over her in a most alarming manner. She stared up at him, wide-eyed.

'Well, I must be off,' he said abruptly. 'But Susan — '

'Yes, doctor?' she breathed, staring at him because he looked all strange and bothered again.

'You've the most honest eyes I've ever seen in my life. Don't you change, will you?' he said at last, and then turned and ran down the stairs without a backward glance. She was left with the feeling that he could have kicked himself for saying that. Why had he said it? He really was the most unusual sort of doctor, she told herself, as she retraced her steps to Elspeth's room. And then she remembered about the forbidden places, and forgot about the Holiday Doctor's odd remarks and the way he could make her sizzle as if she had had an electric shock, just by casually touching her chin.

Elspeth worried her dreadfully. Merida had brought her a gift, too, and had distributed the presents to all the children with just the right air of casualness. Colin even showed a little of the secret delight he felt about the cine camera, and Frankie was thrilled with his tape recorder, but Elspeth was too unwell to bother to undo hers.

It lay in its beautiful gift box on the dressing-table, and not even Merida's gay 'It's something to wear, honey, to make you feel glamorous!' could elicit any excitement in Elspeth.

'Am I ever going to get well?' she whispered to Susan.

'Of course you are, silly poppet!' Susan said firmly, but she reflected as she said it that the Holiday Doctor had given her no such assurance about the child. In fact, he had intimated that if Elspeth didn't improve soon, he would feel rather inclined to have a second opinion.

'What's the matter with me?' Elspeth demanded.

'Just sort of run down,' Susan said vaguely. 'If you ask me, you haven't been eating enough of the right things for ages.'

'I heard Mrs. Boffin say that it might be a bug I'd picked up, in the Middle East.'

'Now how can you hear Mrs. Boffin's voice up here?' Susan said in exasperation. 'Not that it matters what she says!'

'It seems to come from the boys' room,' Elspeth said after a while. 'I wondered about that, because Mrs. Boffin only comes up to make their beds and tidy up and there isn't anyone with her usually, but now I come to think of it, there was a man's voice answering her.'

'What did he say, Elspeth?' Susan breathed. She was so afraid it might have been Gerald Adams. He was the only one who could reasonably discuss Elspeth's illness with anyone in the house.

'I don't know. It was a sort of low rumbling. As if he were standing a long way away.'

Susan thought about it on and off during the day. It had taken quite a long time to assure Elspeth that she hadn't picked up anything in the Middle East, but the more she talked about it, the more Susan wondered if that might be the case. It began to worry her, and that evening when she went out to try and find the boys and Linda, and she passed Dr. Adams' surgery, it was too much of a temptation and she slipped in.

Surgery was almost over. The last patient was already in there. It was seven o'clock and somehow Susan had to convince the children that they must not keep Mrs. Boffin waiting like this for supper. It was the third time they had done it and she was threatening to write to Uncle Damien about it.

Susan didn't recognize the woman he was letting out, but she recognized Susan. Everyone knew by sight the young family staying at The White House.

Dr. Adams said, 'Why, Susan, is anything wrong? Come along in!' and the patient heard, as she went quietly out and shut the door behind her, the glad note in his voice; a note he was quite unaware of himself.

Susan said, sitting down in the chair he had indicated, 'I shouldn't have come. I know how busy you are, but I was so worried. It's something Elspeth said, and it's upset her, I think. I did my best to calm her down but I don't think I really managed it!'

'What was it she said?' he asked gently.

'She said she was afraid she had picked up a bug in the Middle East.'

Susan broke off in surprise as his face changed. 'It isn't, is it?' she gasped.

'No! No, I don't honestly think so, but this has come up before, recently. I'll tell you about that in a minute. First, how was it Elspeth got the idea about it?'

'She said she heard Mrs. Boffin saying it to someone!'

Now he was frankly astonished. 'Well, Mrs. Boffin did — to me! But how could Elspeth have heard us? We were in the kitchen. This morning. You'd shown me halfway down the stairs when Elspeth called, remember? So I sent you back and said I'd let myself out. But Mrs. Boffin called me into the kitchen and insisted on giving me a cup of coffee and then plying me with questions. I said (and I repeat this to you now, my dear!) I do not think it is any such thing that is wrong with Elspeth.'

'She said she could hear a man's voice in the distance but it was a low rumble. She thought it was coming from the boys' room. But how could it be, if you were both in the kitchen?'

'I don't know, but we ought to get to the bottom of this. Where are the boys?'

'I don't know, I don't know!' Susan said distractedly. 'I've come out to find them. Mrs. Boffin is livid — she hates to be kept waiting to dish up a meal!'

'I'll go with you and help you find them, and I'll tell them a thing or two for worrying you like this!' he said, and he locked the surgery and took Susan by the arm, talking to her as he went.

When he set out to talk calm and reason into a person he did it whole-heartedly, no less with Susan just then, so he really didn't see his recent patient standing talking to two other women, but Susan did. She noticed how they broke off their conversation to stare at herself and the doctor as they got into his car and drove away.

He drove all round Holland Green but there was no sign of the boys and Linda. 'Where to now?' he murmured, as he pulled up by a stile that led across a field to the back of Willenfield Woods.

Susan stared at the densely-packed trees on the horizon. She remembered so vividly how she and Merida and Lauretta had gone there, pushing their way through the drunken fences, playing games among the dells and the great fox-holes. There had been no sense of being caught there with the fall of darkness or a sudden thunderstorm; just a gloriously happy carefree sense of being young and having no responsibilities. Were the children there?

'Of course,' she said, as if to bolster her ego, 'two of them are boys — it isn't even as if they were all girls, as we were!'

'It's different now,' Dr. Adams growled. 'The woods are no fit place for young children, and after all, Colin is only ten, the eldest of the three of them!'

'What's so different about it now?' she asked, looking up at him. 'You mean the owner keeps armed game-keepers?'

He stared down at her, almost as if he were on the point of telling her, then he shrugged and said, 'Let's push on to the nearest callbox. We'll telephone to see if the scamps are home, before we think again.'

Darkness was softly falling. The murky, half-misty gloom of a summer evening in heavily-wooded country. Not so much darkness falling as that the daylight was being drained away, leaving a seeping greyness, Susan thought, and she was aware of a heightened sense of being one with all this. It was because he was there beside her, she supposed. Only those two, and a lone cyclist a little ahead of them. The man must have passed them when they had been staring so intently at each other.

As they passed the cyclist, Susan saw it was not a man but a woman, and she was looking at Susan as if she knew her.

They couldn't find a callbox that was in order after all, so they drove home, and there were the children, just finished supper and looking all innocent. Even Merida was there. She looked thoughtfully at the doctor, and so did Mrs.

Boffin and Alf Dinning, under the cover of the children's shrill voices, saying what they had been doing that day.

Susan was really cross. Even after Gerald Adams had gone and she sat down to her meal, she couldn't shake off her crossness at them, nor the sense of having done something she would be sorry for. And yet, after all, what had she done? Merely gone to the one logical person who could answer her question about Elspeth, and accepted his help to look for the children. Yet she remembered, clearly now, the gossiping women, the woman on the bicycle in the lane.

Scolding the children was no use. They received her scolding stoically and politely, and even promised they wouldn't be late again for supper, a promise she felt would have been better left unmade. Such a rash promise from those three! And Elspeth was uneasy, which was worse.

Being such a hot night, it was difficult for anyone to get to sleep. There were movements in the boys' room long after Susan had started to be drowsy. If she had been alone she would have thumped on the wall, but Elspeth was breathing quietly, presumably asleep for the first time for hours, so Susan just lay and fumed. She dropped off finally into an uneasy sleep.

She dreamed of the boys and the doctor, of Merida and a man without a face, and even in her dream Susan was aware that she hadn't spoken to Dr. Adams about this Peregrine person and she had meant to. And there were voices, such logical realistic conversations. The one about Elspeth and the 'bug' picked up in the Middle East — hideous, that one, because it was exactly as Elspeth had reported it that morning. And one that had a curious lasting flavour even after Susan had awakened. 'It's this last four years that the damage has been done,' Mrs. Boffin was saying. Well, it was her voice Susan thought in amazement. 'It's not right, him fetching 'em here.'

And then Susan realized she was awake and that the voice wasn't in the dream at all, and that something was gripping her wrist tightly. It was Elspeth's thin little hand, cold, as it usually was, and Elspeth was up in bed on one elbow, anxious in case Susan should cry out. And Mrs. Boffin's voice was going on and on:

'It's not right, him fetching 'em here. I tell you straight, I never feel safe! Disgraceful — and his brother such a nice man. Prisoners, indeed! Who'd think his brother was a High Court Judge? You never know what's going on at Yoxbrook Manor since *he's* been there!'

Susan reached out and found her big powerful torch and put it on. Elspeth was putting a finger to her lips, for the voices were coming from the boys' room and now it was a man. Who, for heaven's sake? Surely it could only be the voice of Inkpen, the chemist.

'How much longer is it going on?' he asked, and there was such agony and intense anger in his voice that Susan thought she must still be dreaming.

'You can't hold this against me for ever!' And someone else, another male voice, but a deep one this time, said impatiently, 'Don't be absurd, man, of course I can!'

Then it was all suddenly silent. Susan stared at Elspeth and Elspeth's young face, white and hungry for sleep, was one big question mark, and she was scared, too.

All at once Frankie's voice nullified all the fears. 'Isn't it smashing?' he squeaked. 'It's smashing, smashing, like the Secret Service!' and Colin's voice, low, because after all, the household was presumably asleep, 'Shut up, Frankie!'

Susan sat up in bed, her long hair all over her shoulders, sleep still filling her eyes, bewilderment pinching her face so that she looked much more young than usual, the child thought.

Susan said sharply to Elspeth: 'What on earth is going on in there?'

Elspeth, still holding on to Susan's wrist, said very kindly in explanation, 'It's the tape recorder.'

5

Susan was furious. She threw back the coverlets to get out of bed. Elspeth asked in an alarmed voice, 'Where are you going, Sue?'

'Into that room to have a straight talk with them!' Susan choked. 'All right, I know I shall have to go all the way down our staircase and up theirs, but I don't care. This is absolutely the end!'

'Please don't!' Elspeth pleaded. 'It'll make a scene. Mrs. Boffin will shout — she hates being wakened before she has to get up. And Alf Dinning will come out in his night-shirt and he scares me. Do you think he's going to marry Mrs. Boffin?'

If she had tried to side-track Susan, she had successfully managed it. 'What on earth are you talking about, Elspeth?'

'It was on the boys' tape only they

scrubbed that bit off because they said it was soppy.'

'What was?' Susan sat on her bed again in exasperation.

'The bit where Alf Dinning asked Mrs. Boffin if she fancied being married again and she said she still had a husband but Alf Dinning said that he'd deserted her all those years ago and they could go to the vicar and explain and he'd see it was all fair and square because if someone deserts someone for so many years, the deserted person can marry again. Alf Dinning went all silly and told her he'd make a wonderful husband and she went all silly and said it was only because she was such a fine cook that he wanted her. The boys were furious and scrubbed it off.'

'That tape recorder has got to go!' Susan said with finality. 'It isn't nice, spying on people. How do they do it, anyway? Surely it has to be very close to the people who are talking?'

'It is,' Elspeth said collectedly. 'Frankie has made a sort of push thing with a box and a long stick stuck through it. He puts the recorder in it and pushes it behind the kitchen curtains from outside. You know Mrs. Boffin's almost always at the sink talking. Sometimes he pushes it round the door. One of these days she'll catch him.'

'How do *you* know all about this?'

'Oh, I lie quietly up here. I've nothing better to do than listen and people forget I'm here, I'm so quiet,' Elspeth said.

'What shall I do?' Susan whispered. 'I've failed you all! I thought I could influence you all to be good and do the right right but you're all of you running wild, doing as you please, and not one of you seems to know right from wrong.'

Elspeth started to cry. 'Oh, my dear,' Susan said, contrite, 'I didn't really mean you. Don't cry. It's just that it's all getting a bit too much for me. I don't think I'd have minded so much if our Holiday Doctor hadn't been here at all. If he'd just gone, and everything had seemed normal — but he's here and nothing seems normal. Things are going on!'

Elspeth had stopped crying, and was lying warm and still like a frightened little animal in the circle of Susan's arms. Susan looked down at her. 'Do *you* know what's going on Elspeth?'

Elspeth hesitated, then she admitted that she did know some of it.

'Then for pity's sake tell me!' Susan said.

'Well, I know that whatever it is, there's an awful lot of money in it and a lot of people are struggling to do what each wants to do and it isn't what other people want. That's what I think I heard.'

'Where? Lying here?' Susan's heart sank. Not more on the tape recorder, surely?

'No,' Elspeth said carefully. 'Don't be cross, but when you were out, I rang my little bell, and I rang and rang, but I couldn't make anyone hear so I went to the bathroom, very carefully. My legs felt so wobbly that I had to sit in the window on the way back. I was curled up small and no one saw me, and the window was open, and I heard this talk.'

'Who was it?' Susan breathed, choosing to ignore the fact that Elspeth had got out of bed without permission. It hadn't been the child's fault.

'I couldn't see. It was two men but I didn't know their voices — at least, I think it was men, only it's hard to tell. Mrs. Boffin's got a strong man's sort of voice, hasn't she? Only it wasn't her — I could see her at the end of the garden picking peas or something.'

'Can you remember just what was said, Elspeth?'

'Yes, I think so. Something about it was bad enough before those children came but now nothing's private, and what with Hibbs' so-called servants all over the place — (what sort of servants are so-called ones, Susan?) — oh, and they mentioned the doctor. They said they couldn't think what he was playing at but they didn't like it!' Elspeth waited breathlessly. 'What do you suppose all that was about, Sue?'

'I haven't the faintest idea, except that Frankie is right when he says there are things going on in this village but my fear is that he probably sparked things off by being such a pest and a little nosey Parker.'

She got back to bed. There was no point in doing anything else now. The boys were quiet, and Elspeth appeared to be falling asleep again, content no doubt because she had got the weight of that confession off her shoulders. But Susan lay for the rest of the night hours thinking over all that, and thinking most of all about Gerald Adams. Could it be possible that he was in all this too? Surely not!

The next day, however, when Gerald Adams came over to see Elspeth, he not only pronounced her a lot better and that she could sit up, but he also said he had telephoned the Colonel and managed to get permission for the children to go into Willenfield Woods. The owner was away, but he was sure it would be all right.

Elspeth exchanged a guilty glance with Susan, over her own recovery. It was clear that she thought her walk to the bathroom had helped her a lot.

Today was one of those days when Susan couldn't manage a private word with Gerald. Merida was hanging around talking to him, and Mrs. Boffin came up and said that if Susan liked to go with the children to the woods this morning, perhaps Mrs. Boffin could have the afternoon and evening off.

'Yes, that's all right,' Susan said at once. 'After all, we shan't be alone. Alf Dinning will be working around somewhere, won't he?'

Mrs. Boffin looked rather put out. 'Well, as a matter of fact, he's got a second-hand car, and he's offered to take me to see my friend, that's if he can get off at the same time as me.'

Susan could feel that Elspeth was trying to catch her eye. So that reputed romance was really true, then! Susan thought it was rather nice. She smiled and said, 'Why not? I think that would be rather good all round. Dinning didn't say he'd got a car when we wanted to be driven somewhere,' she couldn't help musing.

'No, well, he didn't have it then, miss. As a matter of fact, he's only picking it up today. Trying it out as you might say.'

Merida's eyes gleamed. After they had all gone downstairs, she said casually, 'Mrs. Boffin forgot to say that Alf has received a present of a second-hand car. It was originally through me, though he doesn't know it. He thinks it's for services rendered to the Lewis's. One must buy a little peace and privacy somehow. I thought it might be rather nice if we got rid of that rather bossy couple — '

'Who, Mrs. Boffin and Alf Dinning? It's a rather expensive way of going about it, isn't it?' Susan protested.

'Not really. Now when we want to be

driven somewhere, we can tip Alf Dinning to do it, can't we?' She didn't think it necessary to add that that way she could be sure that Dr. Adams wouldn't have an excuse to drive Susan and the children about so much. She didn't want Gerald Adams for herself particularly, but she hated to see Susan getting along so well with him.

'But why couldn't you have bought your own car, and asked Alf Dinning to drive it for you? He'd have liked chauffeur duty in a good new car!' Susan asked blankly.

'And have him report to my father? Not likely,' Merida said. 'Besides, I have other plans. Never you mind. Meantime we shall be gloriously alone today so I've asked my friends home to tea. Don't look so alarmed — I shall not allow them to raid the kitchen and cause Mrs. Boffin to blow her top when she returns. I've no doubt while you're getting tea for yourself and the children, you could get us some tea as well!'

'Who are your friends?' Susan asked carefully.

Merida shrugged. 'Peregrine, and of course Lauretta.'

Peregrine. At last Susan was going to see what this friend of Merida's was like, and if he wasn't too bad, perhaps there would be a bit of peace for Susan herself.

She agreed about getting tea, and suggested that Merida should go down to the shops and buy some French pastries and anything else she wanted, because it wouldn't do to attempt any cooking in Mrs. Boffin's pristine stove.

After Merida had gone, Elspeth said in her clear little voice, 'Isn't it a bit odd, Alf Dinning thinking it all right to be *given* a car by someone? Even an old one? And what do 'services rendered' mean?'

Susan stared. 'Oh, Elspeth, can anyone keep anything from you? You catch on far too quickly! I was just wondering that myself — what Alf Dinning had been up to, to think it all right to be made a present of a second-hand car. Perhaps it's something to do with his putting up for the Council, though,' she said, thinking. 'Yes, that might well be the answer.' But a present of even a second-hand car!

It nagged at her. She couldn't think of anything else all that morning. She had wanted to go back to Willenfield Woods because of the nostalgic pleasure it held for her, and the boys and Linda were wild with delight. Linda had the transistor with her, and Colin was taking cine pictures wherever he went. Frankie carried the little tape recorder because, Susan suspected, he was afraid to leave it behind. He said innocently that he wanted to tape bird noises, but there was a fight almost at once because of the noise of Linda's transistor. Susan had to settle it by allowing first one and then the other to have a 'turn' lasting fifteen minutes. That at least ensured quiet with Linda's transistor turned off at intervals.

But it didn't last, and in the end

Susan gave them permission to split up and put a distance between each other. 'But be careful of traps! You're not used to English woods!' she warned them.

After they had gone, and the last sounds of their shrill young voices had died away, Susan sat in a warm hollow. The smell of the woods, dank and peaty, brought out by the dry warmth of the day, assailed her nostrils. If she could close her eyes she could imagine herself back four years, hiding in this same hollow (or one very much like it) and waiting for Merida and Lauretta to find her. But that day they hadn't come. They had found two boys on bicycles and stayed by the roadside flirting with them. Merida at thirteen had looked every bit as old as Lauretta, who had been almost fifteen at the time.

The heat haze shimmered. A squirrel ran up a tree, noticed Susan and chattered angrily at her. Small insects moved stealthily among the blades of grass near her. A mole moved, so slowly, unafraid because she was so still. Her eyelids drooped, and she gave herself up to thinking about Gerald Adams. Let all the other problems slide, she told herself; just think about him and what it would be like if he could drop that curious barrier of restraint that was never far away, and discuss everything openly with her. She would ask him what could be done about Elspeth, for quite clearly the child wouldn't be fit to be sent away to a boarding school with the others. She needed careful handling, good nursing, much care so that there was no repeat of this relapse.

But Elspeth would only clamour for Gerald Adams as a father. With that child, it wasn't just a whim, it amounted to a deep-seated desire that had become literally a passion. There was, as she said, nothing else she wanted. And that wouldn't do.

Far away in the distance, above the buzzing of insects, there was a shout. That would be Frankie, letting off steam.

And then there were other shouts, a man's voice, and a sound like Linda's shrill scream. Nearer, the clop-clop of horses' hooves.

Susan's eyes jerked open and she tried to scramble to her feet, but one heel had caught between two roots. She struggled to free it and was aware that the horse was near, slowly approaching. She looked dazedly, against the bright sunlight threading through the branches overhead, and there was the horse, a great bay mare, and a girl sitting easily astride the animal.

The girl was impeccably dressed. This was no rider on a hack from the local stables, in soiled jeans and shabby jersey. Susan racked her brains to think who could wear a silk shirt like that, and brand-new jodhpurs, footwear so polished that the leather gleamed. A too-smart turn-out for the country, and under the velvet crash helmet was a hair-set that wasn't of Quenningwell. Susan was aware that, for once, she sympathized with Linda and her 'hates'.

Susan hated this girl.

The girl said, 'Aren't you aware that these woods are private?' It was one of those cold, perfect voices; not too deep, not too light, not too anything, and certainly with no hint of warmth in it, not even the warmth of anger. Her cold grey eyes stared out of a very pretty face at Susan, with no great liking.

Susan said, 'We have permission to be here. Dr. Adams got it from Colonel Travers.'

'Dr. Adams did? Really, how interesting,' the girl drawled. 'I shall have to see him about that, for the woods don't happen to belong to him. They belong to us.'

This, then, was the Miss Travers mentioned by Mrs. Kimpster, Susan thought.

And at that moment, from different directions, came the children, each lugged by an adult. A gamekeeper had the squirming Frankie, but an elderly man with a rather fine head and grey hair, marched Linda along, and he appeared to have confiscated her transistor. An indignant Colin was in the company of another man. The older man was obviously Colonel Travers. The girl on the horse referred to the other man as Uncle Robert, and she appeared to be enjoying all this in a cool, detached way.

Susan said angrily, 'Please leave those children alone! We haven't done anything wrong — '

'You clearly haven't all the facts,' the man called Uncle Robert remarked. He was a biggish man around forty, with a rather rakish air that was curiously mingled with an air of authority. The rather seedy-looking gamekeeper referred to him and not to the Colonel, when he demanded the evidence. This appeared to be Colin's cine camera.

'Well, what's wrong with that?' Susan said heatedly. 'Each of the children had a gift and Dr. Adams suggested we come into the woods for the morning and he said he had had Colonel Travers' okay on that. We used to come here, four years ago, and no one stopped us then!'

'Four years ago it was all rather different,' the man said.

'Don't I know it!' Susan flared.

'What does that mean, exactly?' he asked icily.

'Four years ago we came here as usual. The White House in the village belongs to us and everyone was nice and let us go where we wanted to. This year everyone hates us and everyone is out to stop us going anywhere — '

The man exchanged a glance with his gamekeeper, who said, 'Mr. Hibbs, will I — ' Susan was surprised to find it wasn't a country voice at all, but a London voice, a winning Cockney voice at that.

Robert Hibbs shook his head. Susan pressed her advantage. 'If you have ever heard of Damien Vengrove, the financier, you will see that we are nice people, not vagrants to be handled this way. Will you let that little boy go!'

Whether the name of Damien Vengrove did it, or for some other reason, Susan didn't know, but suddenly they were all released, and Robert Hibbs said he would walk them out of the wood. The girl on the horse couldn't resist saying, 'And next time you're caught, please don't say Dr. Adams let you come!' And she turned her horse's head and galloped back through the woods.

Frankie didn't seem at all put out by his adventure, though Linda looked sullen till she received back her transistor. Colin marched stolidly along, looking ahead and saying nothing, and Susan was frankly uneasy. As they got through the gap in the fence, Robert Hibbs looked thoughtfully at her and said, 'I well remember what it was like when I was a boy. Life was highly coloured. It was a point of honour to relieve every tree in every orchard of its fruit, and it wasn't stealing. There wasn't a scrap of woodland or a cave on the beach which didn't hold buried treasure, and all the crimes in the calendar were just waiting for me to wade in and put everything right, with guns and swords at the ready.'

He permitted the ghost of a smile to touch his dark face, and he nodded to his gamekeeper to go. When the man had left them, he said, 'Now, I'll tell you this. For every mystery you children think you've stumbled on, there is a reasonable explanation. And for your sister's benefit — '

He looked at Susan and paused, waiting to be corrected but no one did. The children weren't saying anything. Susan knew what that look on their faces meant. This man wasn't going to get anywhere with his 'reasonable explanations'. Still the one he next proceeded to give them did shake Susan quite a lot.

' — I will tell you all, while you're collected together so that none of you can enlarge or alter the story, there are people here who have served prison sentences. Ex-prisoners, you understand, in my employ! And I don't want them harried or persecuted! Is that clear? A man is punished and serves his sentence and he deserves a fresh start, but it's often quite a problem to find anyone who will give him that start. No one wants a man working for them who has seen the inside of a prison, it seems, but I'm different. I will give him that start. Don't interfere with my work!'

Susan was very much affected. 'I'm sorry!' she stammered. 'I really didn't know. I think that's marvellous of you. Of course we won't — '

'Oh, but you will, if you don't keep away from here,' he took her up quickly. 'A loud transistor disturbs the game and upsets my gamekeepers who are new to the job and don't understand the countryside. I don't particularly want their sensibilities upset, either, by being photographed with a cine camera. You will understand that a man with that sort of past can be rather touchy. The same applies to a tape recorder. If you want to know where you can take these children to wear off their animal spirits, I shall be pleased to give you a list of entertaining places, public places. But please keep them off my land, my private land.'

'Well!' Susan exploded, when they had put a reliable distance between themselves and Robert Hibbs. 'Well, I've never been spoken to like that in my life before! And to think the Holiday Doctor said it was all right for us to go there! So much for his marvellous fixing of things!'

Frankie said dreamily, 'That ole Hibbs talked an awful lot but it's only a bit true. I know lots of things that's going on that didn't ought to be! In those woods,' he added for good measure.

'Frankie, your grammar!' Susan said scandalized. 'As for your tall stories, I just don't want to hear any more. We've had the Arabs explained away satisfactorily, and now this business. So stop it, Frankie!'

Still, she went home with a lighter heart, even if she was still smarting at the embarrassing scene when the children had been caught and brought back.

Merida had a new dress on, and looked very sweet and amenable at lunch. Mrs. Boffin startled Susan at first, appearing all in black, but this, it appeared, was her best going-out clothes. She thought unrelieved black was rather becoming, even if she did wear a savage mixture of purple, green and red in working hours. As for Alf Dinning, for the first time he had a collar and tie on; a stiff collar that bothered his throat and caused him to keep pulling at it.

They went off with a great deal of ceremony after lunch had been cleared away. The car, an elderly but 'doctored' saloon, left the village with dignity, and hardly a murmur. It was, whatever it looked like, in perfect running order, and Mrs. Boffin was bristling with pride. There would be gossip about this in the village, Susan thought with some amusement.

Peregrine turned up with Lauretta in a very smart new car. He was, as Susan had feared, a smooth young man. Too pleasant, too cool, but there was nothing much she could object to really, because he was, after all, Lauretta's friend, not really Merida's, and he was so nice to everyone.

Merida had bought masses of fancy things to eat, wisely seeing that they would keep the children busy, even if the adults ate little. For Susan she had remembered to buy crumpets and they toasted them on the grill and had tea in the kitchen.

Merida personally did the toasting, which should have made Susan suspicious. Merida didn't usually remember to do something for someone else. She managed to look so elegant doing the job; her beautifully manicured hands with their pearl-painted nails, somehow looked all wrong as she cut bread and held it to the heat. Susan said, 'I'll do that — you go and sit down!' but Merida wouldn't relinquish the job.

Susan decided it was for Peregrine's benefit, to show him that Merida was really domesticated, although she looked so beautifully turned out, so she supervised the spreading of Linda's jam so that a whole pot wouldn't be used up at once — a thing which annoyed Mrs. Boffin very much, her being of a frugal turn of mind.

Merida said casually, 'Sue, you know Jotham Court, don't you? Didn't we pass it on a bus once?'

Susan thought, and remembered vaguely a great white flat-fronted house with austere wings, and stark tidy lawns and no trees. 'It was beyond Yoxbrook, wasn't it? The other side of the Creek?'

'That's right, we went over the bridge that got washed away the year after in that freak storm,' Merida said collectedly.

'What about Jotham Court?' Susan asked suspiciously. Anyone living there would need a fortune to keep it up, and so they wouldn't be likely to be in the income bracket of even Merida and her father.

'Peregrine's aunt lives there,' Merida said with a smile. 'You'll remember, his name is Jotham, too.'

Susan looked in bewilderment at Peregrine. 'Oh, I see,' she said. 'How nice!' And what was he doing here, she thought, in this holiday cottage, and how had Lauretta (who hadn't two

157

pence to rub together, as Mrs. Boffin would say!) met him in the first place? The people at Jotham Court moved with the yachting set farther down the coast.

'And he knows Colonel Travers,' Merida said, that little smile of gentle malice playing round her mouth. 'Colonel Travers is a friend of his aunt and uncle.'

'I see,' Susan said politely, but she didn't see. She didn't see at all what Lauretta's boy-friend's family history could possibly mean to her.

Merida understood that she couldn't see. She took pains to make Susan see. 'And Colonel Travers' daughter Iris is great friends with Peregrine's cousin Sarah.'

'Colonel Travers' daughter?' Susan frowned. 'Oh, yes, the rather ill-mannered girl on the horse, who got us chased out of Willenfield Woods, even though Dr. Adams had spoken to the Colonel about it!'

Now Merida was happy. It was all

just as she wanted it. She exchanged a fleeting smile with Peregrine and Lauretta. 'That's right,' she agreed. 'I thought you would have met her by now. I couldn't think how you hadn't met Dr. Adams' fiancée yet, somehow.'

6

It hit Susan between the eyes, and yet it shouldn't have done. Even as she repeated blankly, 'Dr. Adams' *fiancée?*' the thought struck her that it really did explain so many things. That restraint about him whenever he was out with Susan, alone. And the way Mrs. Boffin kept saying that he shouldn't do it, and whatever was he thinking of, and things like that.

'Didn't you *know?*' Merida murmured. The kitten who had been at the cream but who was sure that no one would spank her because everyone liked her so much.

'I'm hardly likely not to know, in this place, where everyone talks about everyone else!' Susan retorted, with a rising of her old spirit. Not for worlds was she going to admit before present company that she didn't know. It worried her in case she had worn her heart on her sleeve, but no harm was done. She could now avoid him with good reason, she supposed. Or keep the children with her. If he wanted to give the children lifts, what harm was there in that? But alone with him? Never again, she promised herself!

The children were quiet, whispering together. Merida said smoothly, 'Well, of course, I know she's only just got back from Paris, but it really was a bit naughty of him, the way he has been mooning around you lately. I mean, people are bound to talk, in this place, as you say, and it really hasn't been fair to you. Well, I don't think so, anyway!'

Linda said suddenly, her young face blazing with one of her 'hates' working up: 'He hasn't been mooning around our Susan! She wouldn't let him do a thing like that! He's just our friend! He gives us lifts and looks after us!'

Frankie added hotly, 'What's wrong with that? What's wrong with being someone's friend? You wouldn't be anyone's friend!'

That was too true to be mere perception. Frankie was just being rude, on Susan's behalf, so Susan gently reminded him of his manners and (to please her only, as she well realized) he apologized. Nothing could be more surly than a forced apology from Frankie.

For the rest of the meal, which he still managed to do justice to, he sat glaring first at Merida and then at her guests, paying particular attention to Peregrine. So much attention, in fact, that he apparently wasn't listening to the adult conversation, which was taking a turn that Susan didn't care for.

Lauretta said languidly, 'Actually, that isn't entirely the unbiased truth. He may well start out to give lifts to the whole party, but regrettably finishes up ã *deux* somewhere, as at the surgery one night recently.'

Susan couldn't stop the colour from rising in her face. Those gossiping women outside! She could see them plainly in her mind's eye even now. 'I'd gone to ask him something about Elspeth,' she protested, hampered by the presence of the children. It was hardly the place to reveal that she had heard something on Frankie's tape recorder.

'Well,' Merida said, sitting down to dry toast and tea with no milk or sugar, 'if it had been me, I would have asked him that when I was seeing him out of the house. I mean, no one can gossip about a chat with a doctor in a house with a lot of other people in it. Most proper.'

'Anyway,' Lauretta put in, 'there's still the rumour about two people in a car in a lane at dusk. Whichever way you look at it, you can't argue round that!'

'We'd gone out to find the children!' Susan said heatedly. 'They'd been in the woods for ages and I was worried!'

'Oh! Was that what it was?' Merida really looked puzzled. 'Oh! I thought it was the night when you two came back looking all guilty, and we'd all finished supper. Even the kids had finished! Mrs. Boffin wasn't pleased! Don't you remember?'

'They'd got back and had their supper while I was out looking for them,' Susan said shortly. Merida said 'Oh,' again and tried to look as if she understood. She really did it very well. Lauretta merely raised her eye-brows, as if she didn't think the excuse was much of an effort, while Peregrine laughed.

It was that laugh of his, a small light laugh, that did it. It said so much, that laugh, as if he suspected her of being light, and deliberately going around with the doctor in hole-and-corner fashion while his fiancée was away.

She said hotly, 'I don't like this. It isn't true, any of it, and your friends don't know me very well and I don't like the way they're looking, Merida. Also, you haven't permission to bring your friends into Mrs. Boffin's kitchen when she's out. That wasn't your father's idea at all. You know very well he doesn't approve — '

Merida's eyes snapped angrily. She knew what Susan was going to say. Damien Vengrove didn't approve of Lauretta and her friends, he never had. Merida said smoothly, 'I know. I doubt if I'll do it again. It was just today, because you've made such a fuss about me seeing people you hadn't met, and this was the only way I could think of that you could meet Peregrine, without having the kids in tow, since you never like to leave them. Well, now you've met Peregrine, so we don't have to come here to tea any more, and I know you won't tell my father any tales, because in the circumstances it wouldn't really be very bright of you, would it?'

On that note, Merida quietly got up and caught the eyes of the other two and they got up, too. 'We're going into Quenningwell, to a show,' Merida said quietly, and they all three said a general good-bye and went out.

Susan sat frustrated. It had all been

so quietly said, so quietly done, that good-bye, that the children hardly appeared to have noticed anything. Doubtful, too, if they had read anything, any sense at all, into Merida's allusions. Certainly Susan doubted if the children realized that Merida had just threatened to tell Uncle Damien that Susan was being gossiped about for being seen in corners with the doctor, who was already engaged to Colonel Travers' daughter.

But if she thought the children didn't sense something was amiss, she was very wrong. Linda said, as soon as they were alone, 'Oh, good, I'm glad they've gone! Now we can finish up the cakes they bought. That Merida, I hate her!'

'Linda, you really ought not to say that about your own cousin,' Susan said automatically, but she was so much put out that she couldn't really hide it. Her hands were shaking, and now the reaction was setting in. Gerald Adams was engaged to that girl on the horse, and he had never mentioned it to

Susan, and surely there had been times when he could very naturally have said something like, 'My fiancée likes those sort of things — you've met Miss Travers, haven't you?' It would have been natural, and kind, too. Susan would have had the opportunity to refuse to be seen in his company so much. Now she would feel terrible every time she went out and people looked at her.

'I wish she wasn't my cousin,' Linda said.

'Yes, and I wish she wouldn't have such rotten friends, like that Peregrine,' Frankie said. 'I know something about him. I'll get it yet, I'll get it,' he stuttered. 'It's something . . . something . . .'

He started to tilt his chair back and forth, as he did when he was trying to remember something, and when Colin roused himself to beg his brother to shut up, Frankie started to snap his fingers, in an effort to induce the elusive memory.

Colin said to Susan, 'All that grown-up talk, it means something bad's going to happen to you, doesn't it?'

Susan eyed him worriedly. He might seem vague, wrapped up in his own tight little world where no one could reach him, but he didn't miss much.

Susan sent Linda and Frankie out to play, while she talked to Colin. When they were alone, she said, 'Here, take this tea-cloth and wipe up while I wash the dishes. Now this business of me — I think people will talk about me. They stand gossiping in the street and you can tell they're talking about someone. But I don't think it will last. They'll find someone else to gossip about. Will you mind while it lasts?'

'Yes. I shall hate it, because you haven't done anything wrong, have you?' he said. And he looked at Susan with such misery in his eyes, she didn't know what to do. He was too big a boy to hug, although he was only ten. He was almost as big as Susan, and his size often made people forget his age. But now he was just young and rather lost. Still grieving for his parents inside, she guessed.

'People might say I had, going around with Dr. Adams, but it wasn't like that, and I didn't know he was engaged or I wouldn't have done it. No one said! And yet, come to think of it, Mrs. Kimpster hinted. She wasn't very nice. Oh, why do people hint? Why don't they say straight out?'

'I don't want people to think badly of you, Susan,' Colin said, rather fiercely. 'I reckon — we all reckon — that you're all right! You'll always be there, won't you? For when we come home from school, I mean?' and he rubbed very energetically at an imaginary spot on the plate that was already dry, clean and shining.

She didn't know that she'd always be there. She didn't know what was going to happen to her. She would have to get work of some sort. Uncle Damien had made it quite clear that she wasn't to expect to stay at home. Even his own daughter wasn't going to be allowed to do that. But wherever Susan was, she must, she knew, somehow, arrange to be at hand for when those school holidays occurred. She couldn't let Colin down. All the children needed her. So she said firmly, 'I shall be there!'

It wasn't enough. Colin said, 'At home, at Uncle Damien's house?'

She couldn't really answer that with truth, either. She guessed, rather more accurately than she knew, that the children would have other arrangements made for them, such as this particular holiday, to get them out from under Damien Vengrove's feet. But she didn't say so. Thoughtfully, as if discussing the matter with Colin, she said, 'I'm thinking of going to train as a nurse. I was wondering which hospital to go to. It just occurs to me that if I were to go to Quenningwell, and you were all to come and stay here, I might manage to get off duty and come over here a lot. Of course, I wouldn't get as many holidays as you would at school. No one at work gets that much holiday a year.'

Colin said fiercely, 'Then why don't

you be a teacher and then you'd get the same sort of holidays as we would!'

And he needed an answer. 'I suppose I could. I suppose I could get some sort of training to teach in an infant school.' A little of the ache in her heart eased. To be near children, it just might be better for her than being a nurse, because before she could become exclusively a children's nurse, she would have to go through what was to her the rather distressing business of nursing sick and injured adults. 'Yes, Colin, I think you have hit on a very bright idea,' and she smiled brilliantly at him.

It satisfied Colin. He smiled back at her, and his smile was always a slow and difficult one, as if he found it an effort to smile. He was almost always looking rather set in the face, which grieved her.

She didn't have much time to consider Colin any more, because Frankie burst in, closely followed by Linda. 'I've got it, I've got it! I said I would and I have! I know him — he's the man I heard behind the wall, him what was saying 'It's going to happen tonight'! Remember? Remember?'

'Calm down, Frankie, calm down and tell me all that very slowly,' Susan said, and because Linda was clamouring too, she sent her up stairs to fetch down Elspeth's tea tray and to see if Elspeth wanted anything. Somehow she would have to dissuade Elspeth from talking confidentially to the doctor, now she had come on this information about his engagement, but she wouldn't have to let Elspeth know about that detail. That would set the child back a great deal!

Frankie obligingly but rather angrily repeated his great news. Susan thought about it, and at last, she said, 'Now look here, what if you did hear him say that? You have blown everything up to such importance when there was nothing to worry about. Yes, you have, and it's no use denying it! And I have to tell you right away that I know what you're doing with that tape recorder, and it's got to stop.'

'How did you know?' Frankie burst out.

'I heard you trying it out, in the middle of the night. It woke me up. I couldn't think what was going on at first. I would certainly have come in to you and had a few things to say, if I hadn't had to go all the way down our stairs and up your stairs, and risk disturbing the whole house! Frankie, Frankie, listen! It may sound full of adventure and thrills to you, but when you come to think of it, it's all got a reasonable explanation!'

'What has?' he demanded, scowling ferociously.

'It doesn't follow that something programmed to happen that night was a wrong thing so much as something the person was planning, to keep secret until the last minute!'

Frankie wasn't impressed. Linda came down with the tray and said, 'Something's going on in this village! I heard some people at church on Sunday say so!'

'You don't hear anything at church!' Susan retorted. 'You take comics to read! I've seen you! You don't listen to the service or anything else!'

Linda went red but insisted that she had heard such a thing said, under someone's breath when they were all standing about in the churchyard, waiting to go home to Sunday lunch. Susan repressed a smile: she knew and understood the impatience of the children.

'Never mind what you heard. I'm quite sure in my own mind that the trouble in this village is Mr. Hibbs' ex-prisoners. He may be a good man in employing them but there are a lot of people about who aren't very happy with such an arrangement.'

'Why?' Frankie demanded. 'I think it's exciting. Real live crooks only over there in the woods.'

'That's exactly it!' Susan said severely. 'Some people are nervous and can't quite believe that someone who steals or does other wrong things ever reforms.'

'Anyway, they're not the only bad ones,'

Frankie said stoutly. 'Dickie Stogden told me that some of the big boys where he lives pinch bicycles and throw bricks through the windows and let the chickens out and tie can's on dogs' tails — '

'*Frankie!* I don't want to hear any more about Dickie Stogden and I don't want to find you going with him. D'you hear?'

Susan was so worked up after that, that she took a walk down the garden to cool off. The heat was dying from the day. It was pleasant there, but she still had to face Elspeth.

Elspeth had heard the rumpus at long distance and she wanted to know what it was all about.

Susan said carefully, 'Well, Merida brought Lauretta home to tea, and her boy-friend — '

'I know. I heard Lauretta in Merida's room. What was Frankie shouting about, Sue?'

'He thinks that Peregrine Jotham's voice is the same as that of the man behind the wall who said it would happen tonight — he doesn't know what was going to happen but he was sure it was something exciting. Elspeth, I've had to tell them I know about the tape recorder activities. I didn't mention you — I just said I'd heard it in the night. I've got to take it away.'

Elspeth said, 'Then you won't know what they're getting up to, Sue.'

'But my dear, I can't pry like that, and it would be prying. You know that! It's bad enough to have them doing it!'

'Dr. Adams came this morning,' Elspeth said. 'While you were all in the woods. He said I might get up tomorrow for an hour.' And she didn't look very happy about it.

'Why, that's wonderful! Then you'll be able to come out with us after all, long before the holiday finishes.' She smiled rallyingly. 'Now I tell you what we'll do! We'll start a sketching club! All right, I know none of us can draw, but it will give us something to do, to try. And I think it might be a good idea if we hired bicycles. Then I wouldn't have the worry of seeing that everyone is there to catch a bus back.'

'But I can't ride a bike,' Elspeth said anxiously.

'I daresay we can get you fixed up on the back of mine, but it's my belief that you'll get strong enough to try. After all, these are country roads. Not like town!'

Elspeth was very doubtful, but Susan had got her teeth into the idea. With bikes, they wouldn't need to accept lifts from the doctor and she was determined to avoid him now, wherever possible.

The boys applauded the idea, and promptly told Susan about two bikes going very cheap that Dickie Stogden knew about. Colin said, 'I've gone off my cine camera — no one lets me use it and anyway, I can't afford to have the films developed, so I could swap it for a bike. Dickie Stogden says so.'

Susan was horrified. 'But that was a present from Merida!'

'So we couldn't tell on her to Uncle Damien.' Colin had no illusions about

Merida's generosity.

They were in Elspeth's room at the time. Elspeth said unexpectedly, 'It doesn't matter, you know. I told Merida I didn't want that silly satin bed-jacket so she took it back and swapped it for these binoculars — they came from the same store.'

She proudly showed a fine pair of binoculars. 'They were what I wanted. It isn't so lonely here now,' Elspeth said.

'I wouldn't have minded a pair like them,' Colin murmured.

'A bike will be more useful for you,' Elspeth told him.

Susan planned whole days out for them. Elspeth didn't mind being alone now she had the binoculars and a new supply of books, and people started coming in from the village to see her. People Susan had met at church. The organist's young sister and Mrs. Kimpster's niece, who was Elspeth's age; the young sister of the girl in the butcher's cash desk, and the vicar's younger daughter.

Elspeth in her quiet way made friends, even from her bed. Mrs. Boffin kept a loose eye on them.

But for Susan the main operation was to avoid Gerald Adams. Now that Elspeth's condition was so much improved, Susan thought this ought to be possible. It wasn't at all easy, however. His work took him all over the place. The day they went on a picnic to Yoxbrook Creek they found him quietly fishing and the children refused to see Susan's frowns in their direction and clamoured to him to let them try his rod and line.

There was the day that Susan took the children to Berwick House for the interest of a sale of furniture, and he was there, bidding for some old-fashioned wooden filing cabinets and a big ungainly bookcase.

He passed them on the road in his car when they were cycling about the countryside and the children betrayed her and insisted on his stopping to hear about their latest exploits.

One day he was called to the farm for

one of the perpetual domestic accidents — this time it was Mrs. Lewis herself who had got scalded at the stove. Furious to think she had done such a thing, when she was always warning others to be careful to avoid tipping the can of water. Susan and the children had been lazing under a hayrick, and he had called Susan in to help him. Fingers inevitably touching, while they worked, sent sparks all up her arms, and with deep chagrin she realized that on that other occasion it had not been accidental, this upset feeling. Any touch from him caused it. She dare not look at him to see if he, too, felt any reaction. She dare not look at Mrs. Lewis to see if she had noticed anything. All she could do was to try and calmly carry out his instructions, and to concentrate on keeping her fingers from bungling the job because of the way her hands were shaking.

And all the time she was aware of the village watching her. The old village, round the church and the house in which they were living.

One day, having left Elspeth with pencils and a plain drawing-book bought in Mrs. Kimpster's shop, and an injunction to try and draw something recognizable, however funny it might look, as a basis from which to start, Susan allowed the younger ones to take her up to the churchyard to see some new mystery they'd unearthed. Colin said nothing but plodded along behind them. It turned out to be a hollow tomb.

Susan couldn't help it; she was as fascinated in this as the children were. It was at the very oldest end of the churchyard, where moulding stones bore hardly visible figures three hundred years old, and names of people whose families were now forgotten. This, the oldest of them all, was a huge oblong of stone, with crumbling coats of arms on the side, and at the back, where a bush had grown so thick as to be almost impenetrable, there was this hole. Not just a hole come by the onslaught of the rains and hail storms of the decades past, but a hole shaped with a pointed top like a church door, and the remains of worn stone steps inside.

Frankie said, 'I read a story once about smugglers hiding their kegs of rum and brandy in a hollow tomb and the vicar was a smuggler as well and I reckon old — '

'Frankie!' Susan said sternly. 'If you say one word against the vicar, you'll be in real trouble. Besides there aren't any smugglers nowadays.'

'Yes, there are, Sue,' Colin said unexpectedly. 'So long as there's Customs and Excise there'll be smuggling going on. Stands to reason!'

'Really, you children!' Susan snorted. 'Well, there's no smuggling here — it's just an old opening in the tomb, probably used at the time of funerals, to take the coffins down, and the door has probably rotted with rain over the centuries. I'm sure that's the reason and we really ought not to be prying here.'

'But you thought it was interesting, Sue, same as us!'

She couldn't deny that, but when Frankie started to wriggle into the hole, she sharply told him to come out. 'It might be dangerous. It will certainly be dirty and damp, and you might find more than you bargain for, in there.'

'Like what, Sue?'

'Oh, I don't know, Frankie. Let's get moving. Yes, quickly!' she said, on a changed note, as she saw Gerald Adams threading his way round the tombstones to get to them. 'Come on!'

'Susan! Don't run away!' he called.

'I'm sorry, we're in an awful hurry,' Susan said, with hot cheeks. She wasn't going to have the village make something out of this meeting! But the children said, 'No, we're not, Sue! We've been dawdling all this time!'

'There you are, you see,' Gerald Adams said, with a smile. 'Someone in this outfit can tell the truth. Why are you avoiding me?' he asked her directly, ignoring the children.

'How is it you always happen to be where we are?' she returned heatedly. 'It's stretching coincidence too far — '

'Did I say it was coincidence? In point of fact, I came purposely. I was looking for you!'

'And you just happened to find us, in this out-of-the-way place? Oh, you can do better than that, Dr. Adams!'

'Susan, what's the matter? What *is* all this? Of course I didn't *happen* to find you — Elspeth told me you'd gone into the churchyard.'

'That won't do! I didn't tell her so — we didn't know ourselves until we started walking.'

'She has a pair of binoculars — she has been watching you.'

'Oh. Those binoculars. Well, now you've found us, what did you want me for?' Susan asked sharply, aware that the children had drifted off, and she couldn't even see them now.

'I wanted to ask you why you were so obviously avoiding me, all of a sudden. It had me rather worried. Have I said something to make you angry?'

She turned on him. 'Well, you really are the limit! I'll tell you why! There's too much gossip about me, and believe me, there wouldn't have been, if I'd known you were engaged to that — that Miss Travers! I only found out quite recently. Why didn't you mention it yourself?'

'Oh, that.' He turned and stared out over the hills, through a gap in the tangled trees. 'I don't know. Honestly I don't know. I suppose I thought you'd hear about it. What's it got to do with anything, though? Can't we be friends?'

'Of course we can't, in a village like this! You know it!'

He leaned on the tomb and knocked out his pipe on the top of some railings. 'Yes, I know it,' he agreed morosely. 'Funny thing, the day you came I suddenly realized that of course you wouldn't be the same or look the same or sound the same. But up till then, when I'd heard that you were all coming back to The White House, I'd looked forward so much to seeing young Susan, with the pigtails that would turn up like U-shapes at each side of a hat that wouldn't stay on straight. The most comical kid you were, and so cheerful and good-natured.'

'What's that got to do with what we're talking about?' she said in a low voice.

'It has a lot to do with it, my dear. You weren't a child any more when you returned after four years, but you were a very nice person indeed, and I wanted to know you better. On my honour there was no more in it than that. I'm so sorry the gossips have made more of it — if they have. Have they truly?'

'They have! They're saying things about us being in the car in the lane that night, when I couldn't find the children, and then they were at home having supper after all. And there was talk about me going to the surgery, too. If only you'd *said* — ' She stared across the churchyard, batting her eyes very quickly to stop the tears that threatened. 'I met her,' she said. 'I didn't know she was your fiancée. She was the one who chased us out of the woods. She — oh, we were all angry.'

'I know,' he said briefly. 'I heard about that. I'm sorry about it, Susan. She just didn't know I'd spoken to her father about it. I've patched it up since. He says he doesn't mind, but all things considered, it might be as well if — '

'Oh, we wouldn't dream of going in the beastly woods again,' Susan choked. 'And please don't try to smooth any other paths for us. It isn't necessary.'

'Don't be like that, my dear. Honestly, Iris didn't know how things were. She does now. I've explained to her about all those other visits years ago. She's a very nice person really.'

'Is she? Well, you would know best about that. I'm not being well-mannered — I know it! I just didn't take to her. But that's neither here nor there. You love her and you ought not to talk to poor Elspeth about — well, about anything else that doesn't agree with that! Oh, this is so embarrassing, but the fact is, poor little Elspeth's so full of the bee in her bonnet, about me, and she misunderstood you, and she thinks the person you care for so much is me. You really must change that point of view with her.'

He looked thoughtfully at Susan. 'Why? It will upset her. You know that. And after all, what does it matter?'

'It does matter!' she returned heatedly. 'You know it does. These children aren't like other children. They've had early grief to struggle with, and they've struggled, and worked out a philosophy for themselves. But it's made them older in the process. You can't expect them to react as other children their age. What I'm working up to is, you've said Elspeth can get up soon, and what's going to happen when she gets about again? What's going to happen before that? Already she's made four or five friends of her own age in the village, and she isn't one to keep her pet ambition to herself. She'll tell them what you've been talking to her about — '

He stared at Susan's flaming cheeks. 'Take it easy! She won't do anything of the sort! She's a good kid. And this is a secret between her and me. She won't tell anyone else, you can depend on that.'

'Secrets! That's what's wrong with this place — it's full of secrets. It never used to be!' she flared.

'Or could it be that you were too young and carefree to notice what was going on under the surface?' he asked quietly. 'I don't know what secrets you think there are now, Susan, but from my experience as a G.P., life is full of secrets. Unimportant to any but the people concerned, but very important to them. Shabby little things they want to keep hidden from others, because every human being does something shabby at some time or other, or if not actually shabby, something he feels doesn't measure up to other people's opinion of him. It's all the same. The trouble comes when energetic young scamps like those boys — those cousins of yours — start dreaming of adventure and turning things over that don't concern them. You think of that, Susan, and try to dissuade the boys to leave well alone!'

Susan was indignant. 'You're on the side of people with things to hide!' she burst out. 'Oh, you're not like I thought you were, at all! You're all different and I'm not sure I like you any more!'

They weren't alone. The muffled footsteps passed very near to them. Mortified, Susan realized that her tone was louder than she had intended. Silently they watched the woman go by.

She was elderly, decently dressed, and she carried a bunch of flowers which she presently laid on a grave and stood there, considering which of the urns she would take back to the tap to fill with water for her flowers. Susan said on a low note, 'Oh, bother, bother — one of your patients?'

He shrugged. 'One of the staff at Yoxbrook Manor, actually. Never mind, it can't be helped. Let's go and find the kids, shall we?'

'No!' Susan said stormily. 'I'll go. I don't want to be seen around with you at all, ever again. And you'd better tell Elspeth why, before she starts badgering me to tell her! She won't be satisfied until she knows.'

He could have told Susan that it would look better if they had drifted off together just as if it had been, as it was, a casual meeting and not something to be ashamed of. But Susan was in no mood to accept advice from him. So he let her go.

If Susan thought that he wasn't taking any notice of the woman by the grave, she was mistaken. He watched her thoughtfully — a decent enough woman, but one with an exaggerated sense of right and wrong. She would talk, he was sure, and if the talk wasn't unkind from her, it would soon take that aspect when it reached exaggerated proportions in the mouths of other people. The newcomers to the village, who weren't really a part of village life and who didn't understand it. He was frankly worried.

He went after Susan to speak to her again but she had gone. She had hustled the children out of the churchyard as though their very lives were in danger.

Mrs. Boffin watched Susan hurry the children in.

'What's up with you lot, lass?' she asked suspiciously.

'Nothing,' Susan said shortly, but the irrepressible Frankie blurted out, 'It's that old Holiday Doctor! Every time he stops to talk to our Sue, she gets all fussed and starts making us go home!'

Mrs. Boffin was torn between feeling a minor triumph because her suspicions had not proved unfounded, and feeling a little glow of warmth that these children should refer to The White House as 'home'. It was, perhaps, only a figure of speech, she decided regretfully, as she looked down into Frankie's intense young face. She let the point go, and considered what Linda was saying.

Susan was trying to shush them but they wouldn't be shushed.

'And she won't listen when we tell her there are things going on here, and there are, there are! Everyone's got secrets, and we want to find out. We don't like secrets!'

Mrs. Boffin became alert. 'Now you look here, young woman, you best mind your own business in this place!'

'We can't,' Linda said, 'because there are bad things going on! In the woods at night!'

'Now how would you know about what goes on in the woods at night?' Mrs. Boffin demanded, her hands on her hips.

'We can see lights moving from our windows, and that old Inkpen says he only sets his camera to watch wild life but I don't believe it!'

Susan stood very still. Mrs. Boffin was obviously very much put out about this, although she was saying very loudly, 'That's right! He's always done it, though why a body should do a thing like that instead of being abed at night, I can't say! But it's not my business!'

193

'There's other things going on in the woods at night, too,' Colin broke in. He didn't often say much and when he did, they listened now. They were getting used to him. 'Frankie says Dickie Stogden told him there were men digging in the woods, and he's seen those prisoners about the place at night.'

Mrs. Boffin and Susan exchanged glances. 'You boys need something active to do, to work off your energies. Well, you can help Dinning in the garden this afternoon. He's always complaining he can do with some help. And you'll get no tea if you don't put in some good work, so mind, now!'

She shoo-ed the children out, and when she and Susan were alone, she said, 'They'd best be kept out of the woods,' and she looked hard at Susan, thinking all the time that Susan's head was filled with nothing but the doctor, who belonged to someone else. A person, in Mrs. Boffin's opinion, who could be rather mean if she was upset. Mrs. Boffin wondered whether it was worth saying so but decided against it. Susan was proud, and reserved, too, when it came to her personal affairs.

'Then you must help me, Mrs. Boffin,' Susan said briskly. 'You must lock their door at night, because I believe they sneak out after everyone's asleep. What can I do about it otherwise?'

'No,' Mrs. Boffin muttered worriedly. 'I know, lass.' She looked thoughtfully at Susan. 'You're young to have all this responsibility, but I suppose you took it on with your eyes wide open.'

'If you mean did Uncle Damien give me a choice, he didn't — but I thought it would be all right. It wasn't *like* this when we were here four years ago. We trespassed all over the woods and Yoxbrook Manor but no one caught us. No one seemed to care! We certainly never got the idea that there was anything wrong in the place, as these children have!'

'No, and nor there isn't!'

'Well, I'm not so sure. Why does

everyone want to chase them out, if there isn't anything going on?' Susan said worriedly.

'No one likes nosey parkers, and those boys are that!'

Susan had to accept that for the time being, but she couldn't help noticing that Mrs. Boffin hurried out to talk very seriously with Alf Dinning, and later on Alf Dinning went into Inkpen's, and stayed there a long time.

Susan herself saw Mrs. Boffin lock the boys in that night. Susan had explained to them why it must be done.

Colin merely said, 'Don't you trust me?'

'I trust you both in everything except slipping out at night,' Susan said firmly. 'The trouble is, I don't seem to be able to make you see that it isn't a harmless pastime and you simply mustn't do it. Be fair, I *am* in charge of you both.'

Elspeth was still awake when Susan began to undress. She said, 'Locks and keys won't keep them in!'

'Now don't *you* start, Elspeth!' Susan

exclaimed. 'You've been very good so far! You're not on their side, surely?' Something in Elspeth's withdrawn countenance made her ask: 'Did they run wild when you all lived in the Middle East?'

Elspeth said, 'We didn't call it running wild. It was just that no one stopped us doing anything. We used to escape from the house and go down into the *soukh* and see the most exciting things happen! We saw people steal things — they do it very smoothly and they don't run away, they just melt into the crowds.'

Susan's heart sank. No one had thought to question the children about the sort of life they had lived before they had come to England. Least of all Uncle Damien, who briefed his secretary to write once a week and send a cheque to meet all expenses, and who occasionally telephoned himself to ask if they were all all right, and didn't really want to hear that they weren't. She sighed and went to the bathroom.

When she came back, Elspeth said,

'You do know, don't you, that the sort of burglaries that Mrs. Boffin reads about in the Sunday papers are happening all round us?'

'Well, they have to happen somewhere,' Susan said, without giving it much attention.

'And you do know that there's a mysterious man meeting that Miss Travers . . . at night, in the woods?'

That really caught Susan's attention. 'Now who told you that?' she asked, exasperated. 'And how do you know it's true?'

'I just thought you'd like to know. I *do* have contact with the outer world!' Elspeth said, with comic dignity.

Susan hid a smile. 'Look, it must be nice for you to have visitors and to listen to all the gossip, but it's my guess that there's poaching going on,' she sighed, 'and the local people shut an eye to it. Also if the chemist likes to spend his night-time hours taking photographs of wild life, he won't want the boys making a noise and disturbing everything. I wouldn't take any notice of the stories, if I were you.'

'And Mr. Hibbs' ex-prisoners go and dig up the soil in the night, and that isn't anything to do with nature study!' Elspeth had the last word on that.

Susan put out the light and reminded Elspeth to say her prayers, and presently there was rhythmic breathing from the other bed. But Susan couldn't sleep. She was worried because she wasn't carrying out Uncle Damien's instructions. She wasn't managing to look after the children, according to his views. And if anything bad happened to them, it would be her fault!

The conviction that something bad was going to happen, coloured her dreams. She dreamed of the whole family being chased into a situation of danger while she stood helplessly, unable to make her legs run to go after them; those legs of hers felt like lead, after the manner of dreams. She awoke to find that something heavy *was* on them: Mrs. Boffin's friend's cat from over the roofs next door. There was a window open, and somewhere not too far away, a window flapped in the light wind.

Elspeth was standing at the window. 'What on earth are you doing out of bed?' Susan demanded. 'You'll catch a chill!'

'No, I won't. It's hot. There's going to be a storm. And the boys are out. I saw them go.'

'Wha-at? But how could they? Mrs. Boffin locked them in!'

'They climbed down the drainpipe,' Elspeth said patiently.

She didn't look the same quiet patient child who had been in bed all this time. She was going to be a little wild thing like the others, Susan thought in dismay, once she was about again.

'Are you sure the boys are out?' she demanded, and when the child nodded, she said, 'Right! Back to bed you go. I'm going out after them, and there's going to be trouble over this tomorrow. I might just telephone Uncle Damien to fetch us all back again and there'll be no more holiday!'

Elspeth quietly got into bed and watched Susan tug on a warm sweater and trousers, socks and shoes. She didn't stop to put her hair up. Those boys had to be fetched back. In the distance there was a low growl of thunder.

There had to be a door unbolted. There were four doors and all the locks needed oiling. Susan grimly struggled with the one leading out to the front of the house, determined to speak to Alf Dinning about it tomorrow. Nothing was going right. It was as if there was a conspiracy against her. Only when she was exhausted with the effort did she recall that she could have got out through Merida's room and down the steps to the garden. She could manage it by being very quiet, so as not to wake Merida. She crept up the stairs again and tried to open Merida's door. It was secured on the inside, but even as she stood there, she traced the banging casement. It was Merida's french window.

The boys out, Merida out. What was she going to do? She felt near tears of frustration. She went to look in Linda's room but Linda's bed was empty as well. She got out of Linda's window and on to the low roof and dropped to the ground, and stood staring about her. What could you do with such children when the elder one didn't set a good example? Susan had never felt so lonely in her life. She ought, she supposed, to wake Mrs. Boffin and Alf Dinning, but what good would it do? She was quite sure that neither of them would go out and help her to look for the boys and Linda. Who else could she ask? Someone who would help her fetch them back without going to the extreme length of telephoning either Uncle Damien or the police, which she knew would be what Mrs. Boffin's and Alf Dinning's instant reaction would be. Then she remembered Alf Dinning wasn't even there.

Well, who, she asked herself, could help her? But her feet were taking her without hesitation to the doctor's house.

It was five minutes' walk again, and when she had reached it, she knew it was no use. His garage was open and his car was out. It would be the Johnson twins arriving at last. She turned back in despair. She would have to try and find them in the woods herself. Such a lunatic thought would never have occurred to her in the day-time but now she was desperate.

Two dogs skirmishing in the road recognized her and decided to tag along at her heels, barking a little when she broke into a run. She would have to run, she told herself, or she would lose her nerve and go back. But the children must be found, and then there was the question of Merida. Susan prayed she was only out dancing with Lauretta and that tiresome Peregrine Jotham. She refused to let her mind dwell on any other explanation for her cousin's absence.

The dogs suddenly decided this was no fun, and deserted her. She could hear their joyous barking receding into the distance. Suddenly a car came round the corner, its headlamps blinding her. In this road there was a pavement on one side only, and no street lamps. It was where the countryside began and the village left off. Susan staggered for a moment, then took a flying leap for safety towards the grass bank on her left.

The car screeched to a standstill and the driver got out, running. At that moment it seemed idiotic that it had to be him, but he was returning from the maternity case. He scooped her up into his arms. 'Susan! For heaven's sake what are you doing out at this time of night?'

Anger swept over her. 'Oh, leave me alone, I'm all right! I just jumped for safety. Do you always tear along like that?'

'I wasn't tearing, lucky for you!' he retorted. 'Well, there don't seem to be any bones broken. Here, let me give you a hand — I'd better run you back!'

He was very angry and she couldn't see why. If anyone had the right to be angry, it was her, she thought, as she fought him off. 'You don't understand — I've got to find them and take them home! I can't go back without them!'

'Who? What are you talking about, Susan?'

'The boys and Linda — they got out of the window,' Susan choked, and to her horror, she burst into tears.

He took her back to the car with him and sat with her, while she cried on his shoulder. It was the silence all around them that penetrated first, and she stopped crying with difficulty, and scrubbed her face ineffectually with a soaked hankie.

'Oh, how stupid, I haven't done that since, since — ' and she broke off, choking again. 'It's this awful feeling of not being able to cope. I thought I'd managed to talk some sense into them last night, and to make sure, I asked

Mrs. Boffin to lock them in and she did. But they got out.'

'How? Did you see them go?' he asked.

She tried to sit up, but his arms were round her, and suddenly she didn't care about Iris Travers being engaged to him. It was nice to lie peacefully in his arms, and to tell him everything. 'It was awful. I'd been dreaming and I woke up to find Elspeth out of bed, at the open window.'

He listened without speaking. When she came to the bit about Merida, he was very angry.

'Yes, well, the first thing to do is to go back and see if they've returned, and if not, to wake Mrs. Boffin and that odd-job man of yours.'

'No, he's not there. I've just remembered — he's staying at his sister's tonight, and anyway, you can't wake Mrs. Boffin. She sleeps like the dead, and if she did get disturbed she'd be in a foul temper and very unco-operative.'

'Not with me, she won't be!' he said

grimly. He took her face in his hand. 'Susan, stop worrying, my dear. You've done your best against rather unfair odds. I'm here to help you.' He started up the car, saying in a tone that brooked no more argument, 'And I'm going to have a talk, not only with those boys, but with your uncle tomorrow. I'll telephone him. He's putting too much responsibility on your shoulders.'

'I wish you wouldn't,' she choked. 'It was just end-of-tether tonight, but I'm all right now. I'd made up my mind to go out and get them and I would have, only it was just the thought of searching the whole woods for them!'

'You can't, of course. How do you know they're in the woods, anyway?' he reminded her. 'They need a man's hand on them.'

'They need a father,' she said. 'Uncle Damien's too remote — he can't give them anything, not like that. I did try, I shall go on trying, to fill the gap. Someone's got to love them, naughty as they are. And I'm sure they're in the woods. It's what they think is going on there — it fascinates them.'

'Well, my dear, we are now passing the woods, and where in all that dark tangle of trees and undergrowth would you start to look for them?' he said, slowing down to emphasize his point. 'No, it's the police, I'm afraid.'

'No, wait, Gerald!' In her anxiety she didn't notice she had used his name. 'There — just going in among the trees again! There they are! I'm sure I saw them! Please stop!'

She hardly waited for him to pull up on the pavement side of the road, before she was out, and racing towards the spot where he himself had seen a movement. By the time he reached her, she had plunged into the dark depths of the trees.

'Susan! Stop — I can't see you!' he shouted. This was lunacy. He had no torch, only the light from the street lamp under which he had pulled up. But he couldn't let Susan go any farther into those dark places alone.

He plunged on alone and pulled up only when he ran into her. She was standing listening. He almost knocked her over and instinctively clutched her, holding her to him. 'Susan! Why — ' he began, when all of a sudden the whole woods seemed to be lit up in a blinding flash.

'What was it?' Susan gasped, as an even deeper darkness replaced it.

Gerald Adams was horrified. He could hardly tell her. But she guessed, suddenly, remembering what the boys had said. 'It's a camera — that was the flash, wasn't it?' she whispered.

7

Iris faced Dr. Adams in the renovated drawing-room at Yoxbrook Manor that afternoon and she was as angry as he was.

'Everyone's talking about it! Why did you have to have anything to *do* with those people?' Iris stormed.

He dug his hands into his pockets. 'Iris, if for no other reason than that they are patients of mine, I was in no position to choose,' he said quietly. 'But I've known them for many years and I like them! As to what happened — '

'You like them! How could you?' Iris retorted. 'Do you know what people are saying? They're saying you're often alone with her in your car. Ted Meldon said his wife was cycling home one night and looked into a car and she was shocked to find it was you, you of all people, and that girl!'

'You should tell your chauffeur not to pass gossip on without he checks on it,' Gerald Adams said coldly. 'I believe I've explained that occasion before, but I'll do it again. We were looking for the children — '

'And I suppose you were both looking for the children last night, in the small hours, in the woods, where it was so dark you couldn't even see you were tripping over the wires of Inkpen's camera fixture!'

'That's right,' Gerald said evenly.

'You're not insulting me by expecting me to believe that story, surely?' she stuttered.

'The children got out of a window after they'd been locked in. Susan takes her responsibilities seriously. She could see no other alternative than to go out and look for them. I ran into her — '

'What a coincidence!'

'If it was, it was a lucky one! I was coming back from a case and I was able to give her a lift. I wouldn't like you or anyone else belonging to me, to be out alone in open country in the dark, nor with that hideous situation looming over them.'

'And you found the children, just like that!'

'No, we were lucky. They were just leaving the woods, and hopped back again to hide till the car went by. They didn't want to be seen, and they've told us since that they thought it was a car coming in search of them. They hoped to get back into the house without being caught.'

She surveyed him silently. At last she said, 'I can see I'm not going to shake you in your story or that I can expect an apology, Gerald. I just do wonder, though, if you know what you and those people have stirred up between you. Uncle Robert is livid! He didn't want anyone in his woods at night and I can't say I blame him!'

'I don't know what your uncle is doing — I don't pretend to have any hope of being told — but he has managed to arouse the suspicions of those children. You know what children are like. They won't leave the thing alone until they find out what's going on. Do *you* know what's going on, Iris?'

'Of course I do! And if you want to know, I'm pretty sick at the thought of those snooping children, myself!' She came and stood close to him, her hostility falling from her, suddenly. 'Gerald, we're quarrelling,' she said.

He stood looking at her, with an unfathomable expression in his eyes. 'Gerald,' she urged, 'do we have to? Do you think I *like* this position? It's those people Uncle Robert employs — why does he have to? They make a sort of atmosphere. Oh, don't look at me like that! I can't just be one of those people who say the poor dears have got to work somewhere! Well, agreed, but do they have to be here? Look at this room!'

She glared at the white walls picked out with gilt on the stucco corner pieces. 'Uncle Robert found some interior decorators among them and thought it would be a marvellous idea to make them do the work instead of calling in an outside firm. He doesn't even begin to guess what it's like, having those men in the house! They're familiar and lazy and somehow sinister.' She shuddered, and waited for him to speak, but he didn't.

'And my father agrees with Uncle Robert! I don't know what's come over my father! It's all very fine to love living in the deep country so much that you can bear to have a hideous old place like this made over for a home, but to insist on others in your family coming here too!'

'You were born here,' Gerald reminded her.

'Yes, but that doesn't mean I'm going to stay here all my life! What is there to do but ride? Don't you feel stifled in this place? And it isn't improved by Uncle Robert's importing those people to work, would you say? Good gracious, just because grandfather was a High Court Judge and pretty stiff with his sentences, it doesn't mean that Uncle Robert has to go berserk and have all the prisoners in this house as staff, does it? That's taking conscience too far, even on behalf of another member of one's family!'

'You've been wanting to say that for a long time, haven't you, Iris? And you dare not say it to your uncle!'

She shrugged. 'I'm sick of the place, and particularly the gossip, and you aren't helping by giving the gossips fodder! What do you want to do — drive us out instead of waiting until we can go decently, to London, to Harley Street?'

'You seem to think that's possible by just waving a wand, my dear,' he said, never taking his eyes off hers.

'I've got another uncle,' she said. 'One who really counts — he's in the medical world, and though you won't admit it, it does matter. It does help!' She laughed in exasperation. 'Gerald, don't stand there shaking your head at me!'

'I don't know how to handle you, my dear,' he said at last, rubbing a hand down the back of his head in despair. 'You won't listen to me, will you, when I keep telling you that I'm not, repeat not, intending to leave Holland Green.'

'That's because you can't see it as a possibility,' she told him firmly. 'You'd be off soon enough, if a chance were offered to you. With my uncle behind you, and the money I shall come into next year — '

'No, my dear,' Gerald repeated. 'I'm just not that kind of person, I suppose. But the fact is, I like working in Holland Green. I don't hope you'll understand it, but I like the work. I like being just a G.P. I'd hate to be a consultant, waiting for the G.P.'s to bring me the work, like your uncle when he took silk, waiting for the solicitors to bring him briefs.'

'It's not like that at all!' Iris flared. She put her arms round his neck. 'Let's not quarrel, Gerald. Let's agree to wait till I've spoken to my uncle and hear what he's got to say about your future, please?'

He gently disentangled her arms. 'No. No, Iris, I don't want my future settled by anyone else. Besides, it's settled. It's going to be here. I like bringing children into the world. I like going to the farms and the schools and knowing personally my patients and their families — '

' — and having the excuse to get that Vengrove girl into your car alone at night — ' she couldn't resist flashing at him.

He coloured. 'That wasn't very nice.'

'Well, it's true, isn't it? Though what she's got that fascinates you so, I can't think! Gerald, I don't understand you — if it was the other girl, the blonde one with the good looks and all the money — goodness, she's even got more money than I shall have! But if it were her, Gerald, I could understand it! But this other girl — !'

'It isn't any use, is it, Iris?'

'What isn't?' She whitened a little

217

and stared wide-eyed at him.

'Us. We're not . . . compatible, I believe the word is. I can't think what made us think we were, you and I.'

'I don't think I know what you're talking about, Gerald.'

'Oh, my dear, don't make it difficult. I'm saying that I don't believe you and I will ever make a 'go' of it. I used to dream of you being a G.P.'s wife and helping in surgery — '

'Don't be silly, darling!'

'No, it was silly, wasn't it? I've only just realized it, since you came back from Paris — '

'You mean, since that girl came here!' Iris retorted.

'Perhaps,' he agreed. 'Comparisons are odious. Let's say I've realized most of all how unfair it would be of me to even expect you to do the things a G.P.'s wife would have to do in a place like Holland Green, because, d'you see, I'd always be hard-up, and my wife's money wouldn't make any difference.'

'Try it, and see,' she urged softly.

218

'No, my dear, I couldn't. That's what I'm trying to tell you. I just couldn't do it to you. It would leave its mark. I've always believed in people admitting when they make a mistake. I have, but it isn't too late to do something about it.'

She broke away from him, backing until her hands rested on the painted bureau behind her. She had never been quite so good-looking, nor, he thought, quite so cold-looking. 'Are you saying, Gerald, that we're no longer engaged? Is that it?'

He nodded. 'It's for the best, can't you see?'

'No,' she said, through her teeth. 'I can't. And we're not going to finish this off by mutual consent, either, because it won't be like that. Not with that girl in it, being talked about by everyone! You might just as well jilt me openly as to ask me to terminate this engagement! Is that what you're going to do?'

'Iris, I didn't say that! Can't we talk it over? My dear, you must see how impossible it is — '

'Do you remember what my father did for you, not so long ago?' she threw at him.

He whitened. 'I shan't ever forget it. But what's that got to do with this?'

'Everything, dear Gerald, just everything, and don't you forget it! Now don't be a silly boy. Fancy wanting to terminate our engagement! Darling boy, I'm the best friend you've got. We're both being very silly. In not so many weeks' time that girl will take those tiresome children out of the district, and we shall be as we were again, and then we can talk about a pleasant future together somewhere nice — all right, not London, if you're so much against it, but certainly a long way away from Uncle Robert's misfits.'

Dr. Adams opened his mouth to say something very firmly to her, but at that moment the door opened and the Colonel came in. 'Why, Gerald, my boy, I didn't expect you here! Have you come to tea? Well, for heaven's sake ring for it, Iris, and what is all this nonsense I hear in the village about Gerald in the woods last night?'

Iris said gaily, 'A lot of nonsense I intend to put a stop to, Father, right away, unless you want to do it, by persuading Uncle Robert to take his peculiar staff of servants elsewhere. It's all their fault that the gossip has cropped up.'

She clung on to Gerald's arm and laughed up into his face. 'Say something, darling! Tell Father that you loathe those peculiar people, too! Or no, perhaps you'd better not, because you're sitting on the fence just now and saying nothing. So let's talk about something else.'

Gerald said stiffly, 'If you both would excuse me, I have got some more calls to make. I could stay to tea another time, perhaps,' and he walked purposefully to the door.

Iris went with him. 'Tonight, darling, for dinner, as usual?' she said, and she smiled. That smile said, don't make me forget to be nice and tell everyone what

221

Father did for you, and now you're jilting me into the bargain.

Gerald said, 'If it's possible,' but it was Iris who kissed him good-bye. He made no move to kiss her.

'Oh, by the way, Gerald,' she said, as he walked down the steps to his car, 'that new doctor on the Estate. Dr. What's-His-Name! Not doing too well, they tell me!'

'I wouldn't know,' Gerald said stiffly.

She smiled and waved, and went inside. No one, watching her, would think that they had had what Gerald would have called the father and mother of all rows, and broken it off.

Susan heard nothing of this. She kept away from the village shops on purpose, but she and Merida had their stand-up fight not long after Gerald Adams had his at the Manor with Iris.

Merida was unexpectedly fierce. 'Look, no one, but no one, is going to tell me what to do, least of all someone who is only twelve little months my senior!'

'I am not telling you what to do!' Susan said in exasperation. 'I am just begging you to let me know if you want to be out late and what time you're going to be home. Have a bit of sense — your father has put me in charge of the lot of you and what would happen if you got involved in an accident or you were taken ill and rushed off to hospital or — or worse?'

'Oh, don't be dramatic!' Merida begged.

'I'm not being dramatic! Look in the papers — just look at last Sunday's papers. There was a girl your age taken into the woods and — '

' — and she was the sort who looked as if she was asking for it,' Merida broke in impatiently, 'and she was walking alone in the dark — the sort of thing *you* were doing, if gossip is to be believed! *I* was being decently conveyed in Peregrine's car to a dinner and dance, *with* Lauretta and a cousin of Perry's — ' Merida finished virtuously.

'Then why didn't you tell me it was

going to be so circumspect?' Susan said wrathfully.

'I don't think I have to tell you anything, dear Susan! If I tell anyone it will be my father, and the goings-on I shall have to tell him are so many that I shan't know where to start! You and that doctor pal of yours caught in a clinch in the flash picture of that nasty little chemist with the comical name. Inkpen, indeed! What sort of a man sets a camera in the woods, and what sort of people get caught in it, necking? *I* don't ever do things like that, and I wouldn't!'

'It wasn't like that!' Susan started, but she couldn't continue, without betraying the children's part in it. Merida in this mood would promptly go on the telephone to her father, and make a lot of it, and the children would gang up against Susan for ever. Above all, she wanted to keep their confidence, especially Elspeth.

Merida grinned. 'No, you can't really talk your way out of that one, can you? Virtuous old Susan who never did anything really bad, has caught it in the neck this time. So it *was* true about you and the doctor in his car in the lane that night! When you both came in and saw the kids were eating supper you both looked as guilty as could be! You have to make your story good, Sue, before you start the evening's fun.'

Susan turned away, filled with chagrin. She had lost Merida now. Without being able to explain, and to make Merida believe it to be the truth, she would never have an ounce of influence over the girl. Well, had she ever? Hadn't Lauretta, discreetly in the background, had more influence over Merida? And had they done anything really questionable after all? Yet Susan couldn't still her fears about the smooth Peregrine Jotham — something was not quite right about him, she was sure.

The next day brought a shock for Susan. A letter came for her, addressed to Miss S. Vengrove. She opened it, and almost fainted to see that it was a bill for fifteen hundred pounds. It was on one of Matthew Nutt's bill-heads, torn out of a perforated book of bills.

Susan looked again at the envelope, and now it did seem as if the scrawled 'S' might almost be intended for a careless 'M'. And then Merida realized that her mail had got into the wrong hands.

It was useless to try and explain so Susan gave it up. 'I'm sorry I opened something for you by mistake, but now that I have, will you kindly tell me what lunacy you've been up to now? It looks an awful lot of money for Matthew Nutt to be asking for, even at the rate you spend.'

'Mind your own business!' Merida said, but she looked rather white. Susan was glad they were in the morning-room. The children were racing in and out of the kitchen and dining-room, and Mrs. Boffin's voice was getting higher with annoyance but at least there was comparative peace here.

Susan said, 'Please yourself, but so far as I know, you've exceeded even your allowance with a whacking great leap. What on earth have you bought with that? An island?'

'Funny!' Merida said. 'If you want to know, it's a — well, a boat, to you.'

'A *boat!*'

'Don't scream at the top of your voice. Yes, it was a bargain — well, I think so. Look, do you know the difference between a 20-footer overall and a 45-ft. sloop?'

'You know jolly well I don't, except that one sounds twice as big as the other. What are they, any way?'

'Oh, never mind. Peregrine must have told Matthew Nutt that I ought to have the *Jasmin*. I wanted the new craft but Peregrine says that sometimes a rebuilt one is a better bargain. Oh, you wouldn't know, anyway, Sue,' but now Merida wasn't angry so much as worried. She chewed her lip and glared down at the bill.

'For heaven's sake, Merida, where is this gem of a boat? I don't know much about craft but at that price it ought to be gold-plated, I should think!'

'I wanted a sailing dinghy, just to start with,' Merida confessed. 'It looked small and manageable, and I'm not much good on the water, but Peregrine picked out this other craft and it really was a smart turn-out, and he sort of made the pace, and it would have looked rather wet to stick to a sailing dinghy after that.'

'May a mere land-lubber enquire how big a sailing dinghy is and how difficult it is to handle?' Susan asked, smiling, but she was frightened. Merida on her own might squander her allowance in smallish items but this was pressure from someone else, a sum of this size! And it had got to stop, for Merida's own sake.

'A sailing dinghy is the smallest of a yacht's own boats, and you usually use it to get out from shore to where the yacht is moored,' Merida said carefully. 'But they also use sailing dinghies for beginners to learn to sail. It isn't that they're unsinkable — there's another thing with a keel — oh, well, you wouldn't know about that. It's unsinkable, anyway, but I didn't want that. I just wanted a sailing dinghy.' She glared at Susan. 'You just dare telephone my father to stop me, and I shall tell him about you in the woods and that flash picture and the doctor.'

'Don't worry,' Susan said with a sigh. 'I'm not likely to do that, and you know it! But I do think your father might very well come down here, so it seems to me that I ought to try and get you out of this one before he arrives.'

'Have you sent for him already?' Merida gasped. 'Just because I go out at night — ? You wait till I tell him — '

'Oh, stop it, Merida! No, I don't mean I've sent for him but someone else might have. Either Mrs. Boffin or the doctor. You must know very well that we're in trouble, all of us, and we haven't been here for half the holiday yet. First Elspeth's illness, and then the kids, and the way they've seemed to upset everyone, and there's the gossip about me — athough I'll never know what sparked that off or how it is there's always someone around at the time to put the wrong construction on everything I do. Oh, be your age, Merida, the doctor's engaged to that girl at Yoxbrook Manor. Didn't you know from the start?'

'Yes *I* knew,' Merida agreed, 'but I didn't think you did, to judge from the way you've been acting.'

'I didn't, at first,' Susan said shortly, 'or I'd have avoided him like the plague, only to be honest, what with Elspeth and one thing and another, I don't see how I could have avoided having to see him sometimes.'

'You really like him, don't you?' Merida said, suddenly becoming aware of it, and not understanding it at all. 'Oh, I know he's good-looking, but he's absolutely no fun at all, and he's absolutely hard-up as can be and never will have any money.'

'How do you know?' Susan said tiredly. 'And what about this bill from

Matthew Nutt?'

Merida scowled. Ever since she had first seen the doctor look at Susan this holiday, she had known he had been over-interested in Susan. It wasn't reasonable. Susan had no right to be able to take a man away from his own fiancée, especially when she was good-loking and important locally and coming into a lot of money. Susan was unattached and hard-up and not really good-looking, but she had got something, a curious fascination that made even Peregrine follow her with his eyes. It was a constant source of irritation to Merida.

She said, in a queer little scared voice, 'Oh, I don't suppose you can do anything, but if only someone could persuade him that it's the dinghy I want, I'd pay for that right away. Blow Peregrine, he's — ' She broke off, not liking to finish that, because it was what really bothered her about most men she met. They didn't really begin to show ardour or deep interest until they realized how much money she had.

'Well, I can try, can't I?' Susan said briskly.

'Why do you want to help me?' Merida asked suspiciously. 'To impress the Holiday Doctor with how good you are to all of us?' It was out, and she had meant it but she was sorry she had said it because Susan took it like a blow but looked so hurt. If only Susan had shouted, washed her hands of it, it would have been different. But you could always insult Susan and get no antagonism, and it didn't satisfy the urge to hurt her.

Susan gathered the children, told Mrs. Boffin she was taking them on the bus to the Creek for the day, and set them making individual packs of food. 'Each carry your own, but I'll carry the flasks in my bag,' Susan said.

Mrs. Boffin looked relieved. 'I'll have a good old wash day if you keep them out of the place till tea-time,' she said. 'Think you can manage them? You know what the Creek's like for danger spots — you went there often enough when you were young!'

'I remember,' Susan said, smiling reminiscently.

Mrs. Boffin watched them go. They had to run for the bus. It was the double decker that went into Quenningwell. Susan said, 'We'll have our lunch at the Creek, and then we'll go back as far as Quenningwell and pick up some more drawing things for Elspeth. She's doing very well,' and she smiled brilliantly at the child. Elspeth always waited for that smile before she smiled back, and even now she was up and about again, it was a haunting smile, as if the child weren't really happy inside.

They had the top deck to themselves, which was as well. None of them could keep still. Frankie demanded, 'Why didn't we go by bike? What's the good of bikes if we don't use them?'

'You use them too much — I never know where you all are, half the time. It's a lucky thing I got Uncle Damien's permission before I got those bikes,' Susan said rather grimly.

'You're mad at us! Is it because of us in the woods? We expected awful trouble and nothing happened,' Linda admitted.

'Disappointed?' Susan retorted. 'Uncle Damien will have plenty to say, I'm sure! No, I didn't tell him, but you won't expect Mrs. Boffin to keep quiet, after all that rumpus! She was mainly cross because she slept through it all.'

Susan wasn't really as happy as she was pretending to be, and the children sensed it. She was desperately worried about what she had set out to do. Matthew Nutt was a withdrawn old man. He wasn't, she noticed as soon as they set eyes on him that day, really in a receptive mood. He was sitting on a bollard, staring out to sea. The children ran screaming up to him: 'Hello, Matthew! Can we go out in one of the old boats? The oldest boat you've got, so's we don't scratch the paint.'

'You will not! What happened last

time, then?' he said in a surly voice, and then he saw Susan and looked confused.

'What did happen last time, and when was last time?' she asked quickly. She knew they had been to the Creek once on their bikes, but she hadn't heard of any boat trip.

'They scraped the paint off one of the new craft just being got ready for the season,' Matthew Nutt said.

Susan said, 'Sit on that low wall, all of you, and get started on your food. Eat it there, where I can see you while I'm talking to Mr. Nutt.'

Talking to Mr. Nutt was even more difficult than she had thought it might be. 'She's only seventeen, and her father doesn't know about this,' Susan wound up, peering anxiously at him to see how he was taking it.

He thought about it a long time. 'It's a lot of money, and young Jotham said she wanted it bad. That craft is a dandy bit of work.'

'Where is it?' Susan breathed, looking

anxiously at a large white yacht at her moorings in mid-stream.

It wasn't that one, it appeared, to Susan's relief, but another, almost as large and expensive-looking, which was being energetically painted and polished. Its brass-work twinkled in the sun. She tried some more persuasion. 'Mr. Nutt, my cousin doesn't understand boats but the others made her feel she was being rather chicken, I gather, by wanting a sailing dinghy to begin with. I know it's a lot to ask, but you'll find someone else to buy it, I'm sure.'

'Not so sure as I will,' Matthew Nutt said, spitting thoughtfully. 'Fair gone on it, they all three of 'em were, too.'

'She's not of age!' Susan said at last.

'I heard she's got all her money now and can do as she likes with it,' Matthew Nutt said. 'Besides, she's signed.'

The children whistled across to Susan, and indicated a tall figure working his way through the miscellany of beached craft to where they stood. Susan flushed painfully with embarrassment. What in

236

the world did Dr. Adams want here?

She said, 'Excuse me, Mr. Nutt. You've got someone else to see you. I'll be back later,' and she slipped behind a big hulk, hoping to evade him, but he had seen her.

'I came as soon as I could,' he said, frowning. 'Where *is* Elspeth?'

'She's over there, and she's perfectly well and happy and I did think that here, of all places, we'd be able to — '

'Keep out of my way?' His smile had no humour in it, but his eyes were searching, as he stood right in her path. 'I was told that you wanted me to follow and see Elspeth.'

'Who told you that? I sent no such message. I wouldn't dream of asking you such a thing!' Susan said heatedly.

'Well, it was one of the children from Martin's Lane. Never mind, it's on my way, and while I'm here, there's something I have to say to you.'

'Please no,' Susan begged. 'We haven't many more weeks here, and anyway, after last night, the chances are that my uncle will take us all away. When we go, the gossip should die down. Don't let it touch you and Miss Travers. You've got your lives to live in this place.'

'Will you let me speak?' he said, mildly. 'Miss Travers doesn't want to stay in this place, and I do, and at the moment there is a state of impasse, which no gossip can hurt. Nothing can do more to us than we've done to ourselves, and it was no fault of yours.'

'I'm sorry,' Susan said.

'Don't be. Now, may I ask what's going to happen about last night? Someone really ought to make those children see that they must not get out of the house after bed-time.'

'Mrs. Boffin's given them what she calls a piece of her mind, but it didn't help. They stood still and politely listened but I think they promptly forgot about it afterwards.'

'Have you said anything to them, Susan?'

'Yes. I told them what could happen to them. They in turn told me a lot of hair-raising things that could have happened to them, according to their private reading of Mrs. Boffin's Sunday newspapers. I feel so helpless.'

'Any use my having a talk with them?' he asked her.

'I don't think so. Elspeth told me they're used to getting out of a bedroom window and going where they want to at night. She said in the Middle East they went to the *soukh*, whatever that is.'

'The market place in the poor quarter,' he explained. 'I agree with you. No one but a father can do much with those kids, and he would have to be a man they admired, too.'

'Yes, even Elspeth and Linda need that,' Susan said. 'I feel honestly that I've failed them. What's going to happen to them? Uncle Damien means well but he just employs people to take his family well out of sight and sound, while he attends to business matters. I know there are a lot of men about like that, but it doesn't help. And that reminds me — what's he going to say when he finds out about Matthew Nutt's bill? Oh, here I go, standing about talking to you, and that wretched Matthew Nutt's looking at us! Now the gossips will have something else to keep them busy.'

'Let them. Listen, Susan, you're getting worked up. You simply must unload your troubles on to someone. What's this business of a bill and Matthew Nutt?'

She looked up into that dark strong face of his, and she gave in. It was, all of a sudden, an enormous relief to get someone else's opinion on this most serious matter of the purchase of the boat. She told Gerald all about it.

'How long has Merida known Jotham?' he asked sharply.

'Since we arrived here. Actually this Peregrine Jotham is supposed to be Lauretta's boy-friend. You remember Lauretta, don't you?'

He did. He mainly remembered a provocative blonde who never, in his hearing, said anything of intelligence or the slightest consequence, but just directed a come-hither look at any male in sight, even the elderly postman and the youngest hand at the Lewis farm — it was all one to her. 'What's she down here for? Does your uncle know?' he asked quickly.

'Of course not! He doesn't approve of her. But what can I do? Tell tales to him? If I did that anyway, Merida would turn things round so that he would finish up by thinking I was merely trying to get her into trouble. And anyway, Lauretta hasn't come to Holland Green, not deliberately. She's staying in Quenningwell, and Merida invited her to tea when Mrs. Boffin had a day off.' She frowned worriedly. It would have to be that day!

'Well, I don't like any of it, but it can't be left to you. Shall I speak to Nutt about this sale of his? I will if you like. I think he'll listen to me.'

If only he'd take the law into his own hands, and not just ask her like that, Susan thought! But then of course she herself had made it difficult for him to take that attitude. She nodded dumbly and went over to join the children while he talked to Matthew. But she wasn't hungry. She poured out some tea and sat sipping it and waiting, hoping against hope that Gerald Adams would be able to move the man to give in.

'What's he come for?' Frankie asked suddenly, with a mouthful of sandwich.

'Dr. Adams said a child ran up to him and said I'd asked him to come after us because Elspeth was ill again,' Susan said.

'But I'm not ill!' Elspeth was so indignant.

'I bet it was that Merida told the kid to do that,' Frankie averred, and Colin, after telling his brother to shut up, endorsed that opinion.

'She wants to make people talk about you, Sue,' he said. 'I think people are daft. I mean, what do they want to talk about you for? Can't they see it's Merida up to her tricks?'

Susan laughed. 'I love you all! You've

got such faith in me! But honestly I don't see what Merida could hope to accomplish by asking the doctor to come after us.' And then quite suddenly she did see. Merida was always making sly little remarks about Susan's flair for keeping out of trouble, almost as if she resented it and wished that Susan could be in trouble just once, for her satisfaction. Well, perhaps Merida thought that the business of the photo in the woods wouldn't come to anything, so a bit more gossip started up might not be so bad. But what a complicated way of going about getting someone into trouble, Susan thought.

'Suppose people did say bad things about you,' Colin said, as if thinking aloud. 'Would someone tell Uncle Damien?'

'That seems to be the idea,' Susan said quietly.

'And then what would happen?' he pursued, thinking, which wasn't usual for him. He liked to let life slip by.

'Well,' Susan said, 'I expect he'd give

me a good dressing-down. I don't suppose we'd be sent for to go to his house because that would be inconvenient for him. No, we'd be allowed to stay the holiday out here, I expect.'

Colin wasn't really satisfied. 'Suppose he sent you away but made us stay here with only old Boffin to look after us?'

'That's possible, I suppose,' Susan had to allow.

Colin was very much put out about that. He stood up, scowling at the others. 'Stop eating! You've stuffed yourselves silly, anyway. Come on, let's go and think this over. Back soon, Sue!'

She nodded absently and let them go. The doctor and Matthew Nutt had walked off to look at the big craft that was to cost so much, and then to examine a little craft, which was presumably a sailing dinghy. It didn't look much bigger than a row boat with a mast and sail, Susan thought.

Later, much later, she put the food away. She was still a little dazed from sitting in the sun, her thoughts far away, her head aching a little from the glare off the water. Gerald Adams came running, Matthew Nutt behind him. There was some shouting, and other people running. Matthew Nutt said, 'If them little varmints have taken out the boat I reckon they have, she leaks, and there's a tricky current in the channel!'

Susan ran with them. There was a mast sticking up out of deep water, half hidden by some reeds. Susan could see Colin threshing out, and Frankie's head. He would be holding his brother up. Susan remembered that Frankie couldn't swim. Linda was making heavy weather against the current. Of Elspeth there was no sign.

8

Uncle Damien didn't come down, even after that disaster. He telephoned to Susan and gave her the dressing-down she had expected, and he said he was sending his secretary down that day to see what was going on. He himself couldn't leave his office as there was a board of directors meeting.

He sounded coldly displeased. 'I put it to you, Susan, this was in the nature of a trial to see how you could cope with a situation. I doubt if you'll be much use in my office, as I had hoped, if you can't hold down four small children, not one of whom is above the age of eleven.'

So that had been the idea! Susan was rather relieved, and much more concerned about whether he had had the gossip reported to him. It didn't appear so. He said, 'I would like to speak to my daughter!' but of course, Merida was out.

So he talked to Mrs. Boffin. She, with one eye on Susan, said, with every sound of sincerity in her voice, 'I don't know what you've heard, sir, but me, I'm not put out about it. They're lively, healthy children. Boys will be boys! You wouldn't like them to be weaklings who never did a thing wrong, I'm sure! Don't you fret, sir! Just leave everything to me. I can assure you I won't let anything come amiss.'

When the telephone was finally put down, Susan said in a hushed little voice, 'Why did you make that speech? You know very well you're fed up with us, you were quite alarmed when the children were brought back, and you above all people, know just what everyone's saying about us!'

Mrs. Boffin put her hands on her hips. 'Now listen here, my girl! You've upset things in this place quite enough, without that uncle of yours coming storming down here. We don't want that! And let me tell you — '

'Just a minute! Who says I've upset things?' Susan said.

'You must know very well what you've done! You and those children! Oh, there was some truth in what I said just now, but if we weren't all in this business, I would have had your uncle down on the dot, and those kids taken off elsewhere to worry someone else.'

'So you *do* know what's going on in the village!' Susan said. 'And you're mixed up in it! Why couldn't you have said so from the first?'

'Why should I? Why should anyone? I've closed an eye to those children's doings for long enough, but now you'll really have to hold 'em down, before they turn up something we none of us shall want turned up.'

'Then why blame me, Mrs. Boffin? What have *I* done?'

'I don't know how you've done it, but you've bewitched the doctor, that's what you've done, miss, and don't pretend to me that you don't know!

There's that cousin of yours going half crazy because she can't stand you getting away with it, without so much as a bit of paint on your face or even a decent rag to your back!'

'You're mad! I've done no such thing!' Susan protested, her cheeks scarlet and her eyes distressed. 'And lately I've done my best to avoid him, since I heard he was engaged!'

'Well, what did you expect? That was about the worst thing you could have done! It just about drove him crazy, after he'd started being keen on you! Perhaps I was wrong,' she said her voice softening. 'I did think at the time that you were playing a little game of your own, but now I'm not so sure. Oh, well, there's nothing we can do about *that*! Now young Elspeth has got herself another chill after that ducking (and how she came to be out of your sight and letting the others take her off in a boat, I can't think!) the doctor'll be in and out of this house all the time. I can see it, that I can!'

'Then you must attend him,' Susan said firmly. 'I know there's gossip, and it's the last thing I wanted. You must see him.'

Mrs. Boffin stood pleating her big white cooking apron. 'Mind you, I'm not saying you wouldn't make him a good wife. Better than the other one — well, of course, she just wants to winkle him out of here where he belongs and is happy, and take him off to a big city, make him a fancy society doctor. Everyone knows that's what she's after! And make no mistake about it, he can't do anything else.'

'What d'you mean, Mrs. Boffin?'

'Why, something happened, since you were all here four years ago. I don't know exactly what, but he needed money, bad, and her father let him have it. Well, she'll hold him to that. He's what she wants, and she won't have it any other way. Very wilful young lady that one.'

'I don't believe he'd let anyone make him do something he didn't want to do, or that he didn't think was right,' Susan said.

'Yes, well, money and the good opinion of people in a small place like this, are what comes first,' Mrs. Boffin said sagely. 'And you'll find that all the things them kids think they've found out about, are simply little things people don't want to come out in the light of day. That's another thing — what them kids are doing. You'll have to keep 'em occupied, so they don't go in the woods again.'

'It's no use talking like that,' Susan said worriedly. 'I know there isn't big drama and mystery in this place and so do you, but they don't. You may not know this but when we first came here Frankie was getting worked up about some men following him, from the Middle East, he said. There was talk of kidnapping. Very lurid! Then it turned out that they were from a side show at the Fair we went to. Don't you see, they're blowing things up into adventure and excitement where none exists, only a reasonable explanation.'

Mrs. Boffin was curiously silent. She stood looking at Susan with the same unfathomable look on her face that Gerald Adams sometimes had. Susan said, 'Well, don't you believe me? There's a hollow grave in the church-yard, and to them that's the haunt of smugglers and other villains. Since they realized the staff of Willenfield and Yoxbrook Manor have been in prison they're talking about country house burglaries and Frankie's latest story is that a man is digging in the woods at night! What's the matter, Mrs. Boffin?'

Mrs. Boffin recovered herself hastily. 'I would have thought that you of all people wouldn't take such a light view of those children in the woods, my girl, after what happened to you! Getting in a photo with the doctor and everyone talking about it! It's a good thing for you that no one has told your uncle yet! What's going to happen if they do?'

It side-tracked Susan. Later, much later, she remembered the look on Mrs.

Boffin's face when the question of someone digging in the woods had been mentioned.

Meantime, she had Elspeth on her hands again. This time Elspeth wasn't so patient in bed. She had had a taste of being out with the others. Even the binoculars didn't interest her. The next that Susan heard about it was that the binoculars had been exchanged for the sort of camera that develops the pictures immediately. Susan was very much disturbed, especially when Frankie borrowed it.

Between avoiding Gerald Adams and keeping an eye on the boys and Linda, and keeping Elspeth amused, the next few days were hectic ones for Susan, and she forgot about what Merida might be doing. Merida turned up for meals in the evening but she was out all day. Susan, her energies bent on her sketching club, discovered that Colin had an aptitude for drawing, that Linda could make recognizable pictures by blotching colour into forms, but that she couldn't draw to save her life. Elspeth was going about it the hard way, following instructions from a book the doctor had brought for her called 'How to Draw in Thirty One Days'.

'I ought to have some more things,' she said worriedly. She was managing to look worried all the time now, Susan noticed, yet when Elspeth had been out with the others she hadn't looked worried at all.

'Make a list,' Susan said recklessly. 'I'll go over to Joan Fraser's art shop in Quenningwell. I meant to, the day we went to see Matthew Nutt.'

'It might cost an awful lot,' Elspeth said, her eyes enormous.

'Well, make the list, and then we'll see,' Susan promised. 'Now who can we leave with you this afternoon while I go out?'

'My four friends are coming,' Elspeth said. 'Mrs. Boffin's going to make lardy cake for tea, and a big Bakewell Tart.'

Elspeth's four friends. Susan was a little uneasy. They would have heard the gossip. She had half a mind to caution Elspeth not to talk about it. But what was the use? If the others wanted to discuss it, what could Susan do about it? And perhaps they would find plenty of other things to talk about.

It was another hot airless day, after the heavy rain. There was a damp element in the air. Susan threw open Elspeth's windows, and felt her forehead anxiously.

'Why can't I get up? I haven't got a cough any more!'

'You shall get up when Dr. Adams says you can. I expect he feels that while you're in bed, you can't get out with the others and fall in any more water, while I'm not looking.'

Susan managed to sound quite gay which satisfied Elspeth, but Susan didn't feel very gay. There was such an ominous sensation in the air. Susan couldn't pin it down. People seemed to be waiting for something to happen. Yet it couldn't concern the children. Frankie, since the woods episode, had been so good it was painful to watch him. He and Colin and Linda went out early every day with boxes and bags and came back with such a convincing load of nature specimens that even Susan was impressed. What could they possibly get up to, while they were so busily collecting?

Susan thought about it all the way on the double-decker bus to Quenningwell. The town, when she arrived, had never seemed so dusty and unfriendly. It was a market day, too, and very crowded. Susan was glad to get into the comparative cool and quiet of Joan Fraser's shop.

It smelt of new paper and lead pencils and the fixative, pungent and not unpleasant, used for setting crayon work. Joan was spraying a pastel sketch at a table near the side window. 'Oh, it's you, Susan!' Joan greeted her, looking up. 'Be with you in a minute. I wondered if I'd see you before Sunday in church.'

Joan was courting the organist in

Holland Green, and although she lived above the shop in Quenningwell, she spent most of her free time at Holy Trinity, doing the flowers, helping the vicar's wife with her innumerable sales of work and jumble sales. The organist was a hard-working young man who taught pupils in his spare time, to make extra to save up for marrying Joan, who also supported her sick mother. But Susan, watching Joan's rather plain face which somehow lit when she was intent on a job, realized that Joan probably knew more of what was going on in Holland Green than she herself did.

At last Joan finished and held the work out to study it. 'I never did care for pastel work but Mother likes it. What d'you think of it?'

It was a not too badly balanced view of the creek at Yoxbrook, with the corner of a building thrusting up through the trees on the one side, and the mast of an incoming yacht on the other. 'I ought to be shot for even trying it,' Joan said, with a laugh. 'But Mother was born on the far side of the creek. She's got an affection for Yoxbrook.'

'It's a very pleasant view,' Susan said. 'I don't know enough about art to judge if it's good or not, but I like it.'

'How are your budding artists coming along?' Joan asked carefully, standing the sketch up against the wall to dry.

Susan told Joan about the children's efforts, and then, rather unwillingly, she said, 'You'll have heard about the boat episode the other day? Elspeth got another chill so she's in bed; better, thank heavens, but more difficult to keep amused this time. She wants this list of things. Are they going to cost the earth?'

Joan took them and whistled. 'Well, you'd better take small quantities of everything. About the children — '

Susan turned troubled eyes to Joan's. 'I don't know what's going to happen. My uncle is furious but he won't remove them, I think, until the end of the holidays. There isn't anywhere else for them to go.'

'Pity,' Joan said.

'You stopped before you said all you intended,' Susan smiled. 'I expect you've heard how unpopular we are in Holland Green.'

'I hear most of what's said there, one way and another,' Joan admitted. 'It seems I appear to be a safe pair of ears to pour out confidences to, because I don't sleep in that hotbed of gossip. It's not a comfortable position to be in, because being based here, in this town, I can see things from a distance, and I get a better picture than you others who are there all the time. Am I making myself clear?'

'I think so,' Susan said slowly. 'You are telling me we ought to go away, but I don't know where to go.'

Joan looked a little oddly at her. 'Haven't you got a boy-friend living a nice comfortable distance away, who could invite you home for a bit?'

'I haven't got a boy-friend,' Susan said shortly. 'Anyway, wherever I went, the children would go with me. I'm determined about that. Joan, they've got no one else who wants them. They are all to be shipped to boarding-schools, even Elspeth, I believe, and it's worrying me sick. She isn't strong.'

'You want to keep her with you!' Joan guessed. 'What are you going to do, by way of a living? Going to be pulled back into the family business as an under-paid secretary?'

'That's a hard way of putting it,' Susan said.

'That's me! Can't keep my mouth shut,' Joan admitted, with a rueful smile. 'But at least you know where you are with me. I was only wondering if you'd be able to have her with you but of course in that case you wouldn't.'

'Don't worry,' Susan said, angrily. 'My uncle has told me in no uncertain terms that I was on trial here, and he hardly feels I'm fit to manage his work and his business contacts if I can't manage four children under eleven years old.'

'Nice of him! So? What will you do? I can't see the benevolent parent of our little Merida keeping you for life. Or were you to be relegated as a general factotum for Merida? We all know how rich she is already.'

Susan coloured. 'I hadn't thought of that aspect,' she said quietly. 'What I really hoped to find was a job with children, preferably in some school where I could have the boys and Linda with me in the school holidays, too.'

Joan swung her legs and stared out of the window. 'You ought to leave Holland Green now, you know. Before things get worse. It's no use looking at me as if I've taken leave of my senses. I know a lot of what's going on and being in business I get to know people. At best they're a shabby lot, though I can't help liking them, faults and all. They're so interesting! Especially the lot in Holland Green. But you're no match for them. They'll eat you alive, you and those kids, you know.'

'But why? Just because I didn't know at first that the Holiday Doctor — I mean, Dr. Adams, was engaged to be married? Well, I know now, and I avoid him where possible.'

'That,' Joan allowed, 'but other things mostly. You and the kids are a real menace to a lot of people. I know you've no idea, but that won't help you. See the corner of that building in the sketch? I could see you didn't recognize it. Well, it's Yoxbrook Manor.'

'*That* is?'

'Yes. As is used to be. I did it from an old photograph to please my mother. It's as she remembered it. It was the corner that caught it in the last war. I don't know what was sheltering in the Creek at the time, but it was bombed, and the manor caught one. The Colonel was away at the time, but his old father was there. The shock hastened his end, people think. What I'm coming to is, what with death duties and one thing and another, the family decided they'd leave that wing as it was. They just couldn't afford to have much done to it.'

'But I didn't see that damage when

we used to play there!'

'No, well, later they had the ruined wing removed and that part sealed off, to make a smaller place to keep going. But someone else died, and there were more death duties, and they packed it in. Moved out into a much smaller house outside this town. The Manor was on the market for years, empty and dirty (as you knew it) and no one expected it to sell. And then the Colonel and dear Iris came back, and opened up a few rooms to live in. Why? That's what everyone is asking.'

'Cheaper than where they were?' Susan guessed, but Joan smiled derisively.

'I doubt it, but at the same time his brother-in-law opened up Willenfield House, also shuttered and on the market, and they brought in, very quietly at first, these prisoners.'

'I heard about that,' Susan said. 'He obviously feels strongly about the grandfather who was a High Court Judge and very severe.'

'Oh, come off it!' Joan begged. 'Well, he might be filled with lots of charitable ideas, but these chappies do have to be paid, even if they can't command the high wages normal staff might be tempted with, even if you could get them. And everyone knows that the only one in that outfit who has any money is Iris and she doesn't inherit yet, and I honestly can't see her stumping up for her father's and uncle's charitable notions. Everyone knows she hates those prisoner chappies, even though they have been doing interior decoration on the Manor at cut rates. She just wants to get out of the place!'

'I don't understand — ' Susan began.

'I know you don't, duckie, but all these details are important because I'm leading up to just what you and those kids are doing. Now don't say you're all doing nothing, because you really don't know what it's all about.'

She paused to serve a customer, while Susan went round examining paint brushes for Elspeth and wondering if it was going to be a nine days' wonder, this sketching business, and money thrown away. When the customer had gone out, Joan turned to her.

'There's a jolly good reason why those two houses were opened up and the woods sealed off. And I'm guessing at it. I could be wrong but I don't think I am. I shall have to trust you, too, but it's for your sake as well. Peter (my bloke, you know) is a realist. No side whatever. He knows jolly well that he'll never save enough for us to get married and keep Mother, on what he gets for being organist, nor from his wooden-headed pupils, so he takes on any little job, so long as it's paid, and he's not strong, so it has to be clerical. He's had some bits of written work flung at him from the high and mighty bods on the local Council, and through it, we discovered that there's an under-cover war going on to take over the Willenfield woods to build another Estate.'

'Oh, no!' Susan was aghast.

'Sentimental, my dear, because you

used to trespass so happily there? It would be a good thing for Holland Green, you know! But for some reason, the Colonel and Robert Hibbs are absolutely against it. Well, now, this is an odd fact among many that keep trickling out. We know that Inkpen, who is on the Council, was mad keen to get this through. Something to do with a relative of his coming up for a contract, building, you know. But much as he wants it, he's holding back. Now why?'

'Don't ask me,' Susan said blankly. 'Perhaps he doesn't want to lose the place he uses for his nature study films?'

'Infant!' Joan scoffed. 'What nature study films? He rigs up the camera, yes, but I very much doubt if that's the purpose. I know, because I tested him out by a few simple nature study questions one day, and he hadn't a clue what I was talking about. No, he's trying to take pictures of something else, but what?'

'Well,' the now-amused Susan said, 'if there's anything to discover, our Frankie will discover it!'

Joan leaned across the counter to her and said very seriously, 'I know! That's just it! And it's dangerous! Susan, those kids are playing at adventure but they're stalking grown people with adult problems, adult stakes! Don't you see? If Inkpen is up to something, he won't let a bunch of kids get in his way. It may seem small stuff to you townies, being a chemist in a place like Holland Green and on the Council, but it's his life.'

'But he wouldn't hurt our children!' Susan breathed.

Joan evaded that remark. She said instead, 'There's another thing. Some years ago there was a country house burglary on our doorstep — at Jotham Court, to be exact!'

'The aunt's place, Peregrine Jotham's aunt?' Susan put in.

'That's it! Well, the stuff was insured, so they didn't lose out, but the burglar in question (Frenwick, his name was) was supposed to have hidden it locally. All right, you're going to laugh at me for weaving tales like your kids do, but it may well be that they've heard, too, that Frenwick has been seen in the district. He got a lot of his time knocked off as remission because he helped to save a warder's life in one of those stupid riots they have. Well, suppose Frenwick has come here to dig up his loot?'

Susan said, 'Oh, now Joan, you're going further than even our Frankie! Well, all I can say is, if Inkpen didn't stop the Council from churning up the woods for their new Estate, everyone would be saved a lot of trouble. The bulldozers would find it for them!'

'For whom?' Joan asked very seriously. 'Doesn't it occur to you, Susan, that there are people about who might not want bulldozers churning up a cache of jewellery from a country house robbery? Frenwick, for example.'

Now Susan was beginning to be worried. 'But if he's the one who stole the stuff, he would know where he buried it, surely? And isn't there something about police keeping an eye on burglars when the loot has never been recovered?'

'In the ordinary way, yes. But there are several ex-burglars in those woods, working as gamekeepers and outdoor staff, all going straight. Frenwick might just reasonably get lost among them, so far as the police are concerned. Anyway, who have we got as police?'

'Dickie Stogden's friend's uncle,' Susan said. 'Well, I know that one. I don't know his sergeant, but Frankie and Colin are friends with the sergeant's own children. I've heard them talking about it.'

'That's right. Now, if I were a small-time copper, I would listen to my kids' chatter, and pick up the useful bits, especially if I were ambitious. Do you think the Holland Green police are ambitious?'

'I don't know,' Susan said blankly. 'Do you?'

'I do indeed! My Peter walks along with your Dickie Stogden's friend's uncle some nights, when he's come late from church — the company, you see.

My Peter often says, that chap's so keen, I'd hate to be at the wrong end of a crime on his beat! See what I mean? I wouldn't be surprised if he doesn't follow the kids into the woods one of these nights, just to see where it leads him.'

'Oh! I had no idea,' Susan said worriedly. 'Still, it may not be so really. Oh, no!' she broke off, in distress.

'What have you remembered?' Joan asked, curiously.

'Frankie and that tape recorder of his,' Susan said without thinking. 'Oh, it might just be nothing, but it might be something serious. I'm trusting you with it, Joan! You see, I've just remembered hearing Mr. Inkpen say something about 'You can't keep me held down like this' (or something like it) and a man's voice said, 'Don't be absurd, man, of course I can!''

'Any idea who the other man was?' Joan breathed.

'No. I've no idea,' Susan lied. But she was such a bad liar. Joan said shrewdly,

'I'm thinking it just might have been the voice of Robert Hibbs. There's something . . . I can't just put my finger on it, but it's something that happened and I think it might have some significance. You see, Robert Hibbs doesn't want his woods churned up. It may just be pride of possession, it might just be that he'd have nothing for his tame game-keepers to work at, or it just might be some other reason. Inkpen is mad keen to get the contract through for that Estate, but he doesn't — and why? Could it just be that Robert Hibbs is the one who is stopping him?'

'That doesn't sound very likely,' Susan said breathlessly.

'Well, I don't know. Suppose Hibbs is the one?'

'Oh, really, aren't we letting our private detective work run away with us?' Susan said uneasily.

'Don't make any mistake about it, my dear, a lot of people would just hate those kids in your care to come snooping too near them. Wait, I've got it! I've remembered! It just about fits, but why, *why?*'

Her face had lit again, with excitement. At such times she was no longer plain. Susan could begin to see a little of what the thin, romantic young organist could see in this girl.

Joan said, 'There was a time once, two or three years ago (can't remember just when!) when Inkpen had had some trouble. We never found out what it was, but it would be money, I suppose. He was so worried, he was frankly vague. He gave me something quite impossible instead of the bottle of cleansing milk I'd asked for. Anyway, this particular evening I was still in the shop, prowling round looking for the brand I wanted. It was no use asking him to get it — and Robert Hibbs came in. Yes, I remember now — I've often wondered what it was about and now I think I see! He slapped a bottle full of medicine on the counter and he said something in a low tone to Inkpen — something like 'I know it's only for my cook, but you must hate her pretty badly to do that!' I still remember the way Inkpen looked. I thought he was going to faint. He looked like death!'

'But I don't understand — why?' Susan breathed.

Joan shrugged. 'You guess is as good as mine, but just suppose, *just suppose* he had mixed the wrong stuff, a lethal dose — if it got out, it could ruin him!'

'What did Mr. Hibbs say? He should have taken some action if that were so, surely?' Susan protested, still not really believing.

'Yes, he should, shouldn't he?' Joan agreed, thinking. 'He stood there looking at Inkpen, and Inkpen muttered something. I suppose he was asking what Hibbs was going to do. I remember Hibbs said, 'Nothing! Don't be a fool, man. Throw that stuff away and pull yourself together!' Well, now, isn't that interesting? I'd almost forgotten it. But it holds together, doesn't it? You're not really with me, you know, Susan! Think — suppose Robert Hibbs knew there was something he wanted to prevent Inkpen from doing, such as getting the woods developed and churning the whole place upside down? Well, if he did Inkpen the little service of not proceeding against him (that's if Inkpen did make a horrid mistake with that medicine during the time he was upset and worried) then of course Inkpen wouldn't dream of pushing his pet dream any further, would he?'

'But isn't there an ugly name for that?' Susan asked.

'This is all supposition, Susan. I might be wrong. It's between you and me,' Joan said quickly, fearing she had put Susan in such a state that she would immediately go and tell someone else about it. 'I just want you to realize how easy it would be for those kids to upset people without realizing why. To say nothing of you getting yourself talked about with the doctor — oh, and talk of the devil, here he is!'

'No! Surely not!' Susan exclaimed, but there was Gerald Adams, walking briskly across the road in a gap in the traffic, carrying his black bag. There was no sign of his car. He must have parked it at the back.

'I'm going,' Susan said, but Gerald Adams gave her no chance to slip away.

'So there you are, Susan! I'll just run up and see your mother, Joan, but hang on to Susan, will you? I particularly want to talk to her afterwards.'

'But my mother's all right now, doctor,' Joan said.

'Never mind. I'm a cautious chap — I like to make sure,' he said, smiling broadly. To Susan he said, 'No, it wasn't a coincidence, me finding you here! I can see you're itching to say it. I came especially. Elspeth told me where you'd be.'

They listened to him running up the stairs. Susan, her face still hot, said, 'There's no reason why I shouldn't escape now, all the same. I'm going to!'

'I wouldn't,' Joan advised. 'At least it looks plausible, his coming here to attend my mother, but if you slip off he'll only go looking for you, and it might not be such a private place where he'd finally track you down. If he really wants to talk to you, he'll keep on till he does find you.'

9

Susan didn't go to church the next morning. Elspeth wasn't so well. Not her chill — she had got over that. But a plain common or garden bilious attack, Mrs. Boffin said scathingly.

'It's her visitors, the little varmints! All brought something sweet and sticky for her, and instead of turning over the cakes to me to dole out, they had a secret party round her bed! I hope the rest of 'em have been sick, too!'

Elspeth stayed alone and in a darkened room all that Sunday, but was well enough to permit Susan to go to evening service.

Evening service was something she had never been to before in Holland Green. It was different, subtly different, in the congregation. These were the women who had been cooking Sunday lunch while morning service was attended by the menfolk and the children. These were the backbone of Holland Green, and, Susan discovered, this congregation was the one where the rumours began and the gossip spread. Too many people looked covertly at her, and then looked significantly towards one pew in the front where Dr. Adams sat. Merida ought to have been with her, Susan thought. But Merida was out with her friends, heaven knew where. Since the affair of the boat had been smoothed out by Gerald Adams, Merida was all cock-a-hoop again.

Susan slipped away quickly afterwards, so that Gerald shouldn't have a chance of speaking to her openly. Susan saw the Colonel and Iris Travers go over to speak to him and she wondered why he hadn't been sitting with them. She could only think that he had come in late and slipped in by the side door and sat on the end of the nearest pew so as not to create a disturbance. Iris Travers, she noticed, wasn't looking very pleased.

Joan joined her suddenly, from the shadows. 'I'll walk back with you and then return to wait for my Peter. People are talking about you — I knew they would! Where did you and the doctor go yesterday, after you left my place?'

'Nowhere,' Susan said promptly. 'At least, he drove me back to Holland Green. He had another visit and dropped me at the bottom end of the High Street. I don't know where he went then.'

'Well, your luck was out. Someone saw you as you got out of his car. I've heard several people talking about it. He didn't sit with the Travers' so they're hazarding guesses about whether you're breaking that romance up ! I wish you'd get a lad of your own. How would it be if Peter found someone to take you around, just till the gossip stops?'

Susan was very angry. 'You mean well, Joan, but there's nothing I have to worry about. I would have refused the lift if I could, but there really didn't seem any harm in it.'

'Don't say I didn't warn you. Even

the nicest people are saying there's no smoke without fire!'

They had reached the gate of The White House. Joan left her, but she looked troubled, Susan noticed.

That was the start of a week that had rather odd repercussions.

It was difficult to say how it all began, but by the end of the week it was clear that Gerald had no more patients. One by one, the surgery had emptied, and (according to Frankie who got it from Dickie Stogden) they were going to the doctor on the new estate. Dickie's mother and grandmother had had to queue outside the surgery; they just couldn't get in.

'But why, why?' Susan asked blankly.

Frankie didn't understand why. He was a bright boy but at eight it is difficult to understand why adults will leave a doctor they know to be good at his work, and go to a new man who is over-worked and doesn't know them, just because there is a rumour going around that their own doctor has been behaving unprofessionally. Still, he repeated it, as he had heard someone saying. Susan understood only too well.

'Colin said it means they're saying bad things about you, Sue!' Frankie said fiercely. And the next time he came in, he had a black eye. 'I told a boy not to say bad things about you and he said his mum was saying it so why shouldn't he? So I blacked his eye too.'

Mrs. Boffin said, 'You'll have to go, you know. You've set this place by the ears, you and Dr. Adams. I wouldn't have believed it of him, him that was all decently engaged to be married to that Miss Travers, and her coming into money and being Colonel Travers' daughter and all. If I were you, I'd talk to your uncle on the telephone.'

'Telling him what you've just said?' Susan murmured. 'It isn't anything we've done, Dr. Adams, and me. You know that!'

Mrs. Boffin looked at Susan consideringly. Susan had subtly altered in these weeks. She had lost the wide-eyed schoolgirl look. For the first time Mrs. Boffin noticed that Susan had good bones; her pale face had the makings of poise and elegance, and there was a warmth about her, a kind of glow, that drew people, and especially children. That, of course, had been there all the time, but coupled with this other thing she had acquired, Mrs. Boffin, without a great fund of words, was the first to admit, to herself at least, that the effect was magnetic.

'Who's going to believe that, besides me?' she thrust, in answer to Susan's question, and when Susan's eyebrows shot up indignantly, Mrs. Boffin shrugged and said, 'You both go about looking as if no one else exists. To look at you both, even across the bed of a sick child, you're both raddled with excitement. Makes a body feel in the way, to be in the very room with you both, that it does. And if you're both like that in this house, what are you both like out of doors? Always meeting up with each other, I hear, and who cares whether it's a good reason or not? You've been seen in his car in the lane at night, and that's good enough, without being seen with him in Quenningwell, in the High Street here, and in the woods, of all places, in the small hours! You ought to have more sense, if nothing else!'

'I see what you mean,' Susan agreed quietly. 'I'll see what I can do about getting somewhere else to go, perhaps somewhere where the children could be with me.'

'Somewhere where the doctor won't be able to find you, neither,' Mrs. Boffin said shortly.

Later, at lunch that day, Mrs. Boffin said, her eyes not meeting anyone's, 'I've got a sister what has a girl starting her first baby. Needs help, she does, and I'm thinking it might be that you'd go and stay with her, Susan. The house isn't all that small — I mean, you could have the children with you.'

Everyone looked up at Mrs. Boffin. Merida drawled, 'Does my father know about this?'

Mrs. Boffin said, 'If Susan's willing, then I shall talk to him on the telephone myself, and it might just be, if I get any sauce from any of you, that I shall give him a full report of each one of you — each one!' she finished for good measure.

Merida said, 'There's no need to tell him anything about me — I shall be doing that myself. But I would like to know if I'm to be included in this — er — pilgrimage !'

'You were not included,' Mrs. Boffin snapped.

'Then we shall have to think again, shan't we, about arrangements for me?' Merida said sweetly.

The children were very quiet. Susan hardly noticed at the time, she was so busy talking to Mrs. Boffin about this unknown niece who had suddenly materialized, needing help from Susan. The children slipped off almost unnoticed as soon as the meal was over, and vanished for the afternoon. Susan sat with Elspeth, helping her with her drawings. 'It's the blind leading the blind, isn't it?' she laughed ruefully. 'I don't seem to be as good at it as you are, pet!'

Elspeth said, 'Never mind the old drawings. What's this about us leaving here? Frankie told me before he went out.'

'Oh, dear. Well, we — that is, Mrs. Boffin and I — think it's for the best. She has a young relative who could do with some help, so I am going, and you'll all come too, of course.'

'She's getting rid of us,' Elspeth said. 'It's because everyone wants us to go, isn't it?'

Susan wanted to say roundly that such a thing wasn't so, but it wasn't any use lying to Elspeth. The child said, 'I don't mind, really, so long as we're with you. But what's Uncle Damien going to say about it?'

'Not much, I imagine, so long as he isn't bothered,' Susan had to admit. This child saw too much altogether!

'I thought so. We're a nuisance to

him. What about Merida, though?'

'Well, she's just as much of a nuisance to anyone,' Susan pointed out. 'He'll be glad if she goes too, I suppose, but I don't think she wants to go with us.'

'It's this business of men, you know,' Elspeth said, with an air of seriousness that was touching and comical. 'Her and that awful Peregrine and you and the doctor. Mind you, I do just wish that you and Dr. Adams could decide to get married, and then we could all be with you and it would be all right. I mean, if he married you, people wouldn't talk — at least, Ann says so, and my other friends say it's awful, everyone talking about it at home, and not knowing what to think, because they really like the doctor. It seems they think he's being unwise. What does that mean?'

'Well, let's put it this way. Doctors, more than other men, are supposed to do the right and proper thing, and set an example. They're not supposed to ask one person to marry them and then be friends with another person, like me.'

'Oh, is that all?' Elspeth said. 'Well, I know what that's all about because I asked him straight out, and it seems that he quite liked that Iris person at first but then you came along and he can quite see that you'd be a better wife for a doctor because you know how to look after children and make people comfortable.'

'He had no business to talk to you like that!' Susan said.

'Don't be furious! He didn't actually mention you. I said, 'Would Miss Travers know how to look after someone like me, and would she be worried about people like Frankie when he gets out in the night?' and he said no, and I said, 'Would Susan make a nice sort of wife for a doctor?' and he said, all sort of angry, that you'd make a very good wife indeed for a doctor. Any doctor. So you see, it was all right, wasn't it?'

Susan sighed, and said, 'Yes, pet, I expect so, but I wish you hadn't said any of those things.'

'Did I do wrong?'

'Well, let's say you didn't make the situation any easier, because I really believe in my heart that he was only saying those things because you wanted him to, and he wants you better.'

'Oh, no,' Elspeth said firmly. 'He's not like that!'

Nothing comforted Susan. There was a lump of misery somewhere inside her that made her wish they'd never come back here. Nothing was improved when she found Merida in her room, crying.

Merida was not the sort of person to shed tears about anything, and she was very much put out that Susan should discover her in that state.

'Whatever's wrong?' Susan asked, and she looked so white and upset that Merida decided against snapping at her, and told her, baldly, so dispassionately indeed that it hurt.

'I've got too much money.'

Susan stared blankly. 'You've never minded before,' she said. 'It's all right about Matthew Nutt — I told you so at the time. Dr. Adams talked to him.'

'You don't begin to see, do you?' Merida cried. 'You and the doctor! At least you know he's so silly over you, just you, that he'll get himself talked about! How would you like it if you had so much money that you wouldn't be sure whether it was you or your money — oh, forget it.'

Susan reeled from the shock. 'You can't be well, to say such things. Dr. Adams is engaged to Miss Travers, and so far as I know, he just wants to be friends with me as he used to be.'

'Don't be so wet!' Merida begged her. 'Unless you're playing some clever game of your own.' She considered the point while she put fresh make-up on her face. 'Well, that could be it, because if he breaks it off with that girl at Yoxbrook, he'll be in the soup good and proper, if he isn't already. Come to think of it, I suppose she could have started the whispering campaign to empty his surgery!' She turned and stared at Susan. 'You can't really be so daft as to think he isn't silly over you? And if he's let her see it, openly, and if the rumour's true that he's broken it off from her, she'll drive him out of this place. She will, you know! And he's so hard up, he'll have nothing, nothing! In fact, he'll be lucky if he doesn't get an enquiry or whatever doctors get when there's gossip about them. Don't you know anything like this? How is it I know my way around and I'm younger than you?'

Susan thought, 'My dear, you might know your way around and you might be frightfully rich, but at this moment you look far from happy!' She said, 'I thought we were talking about you, Merida. Don't be in a hurry to jump into marriage. Have a good time first, for heaven's sake. I don't believe people get much of a good time after they're married. There are so many worries attached to loving people.'

The moment had slipped away, however, and Merida was sorry she had said anything. She finished her face and settled down to removing her nail varnish, which, Susan had discovered, could take ages. 'Are you going out tonight, Merida?'

'Why?' Merida asked guardedly.

'You remember what I said. I don't mind, so long as I know who you're with and where you'll be. That's only fair.'

'All right. I shall be with a party which, you'll be glad to know, includes Lauretta and Peregrine, and we're going to a new place on the London road beyond Quenningwell, which I hear is pretty lush and has a super swimming pool. Want to see my new swimsuit?' And she showed Susan a most impractical-looking garment in yellow and gold, which must have cost the earth.

Afterwards, Susan wondered why she hadn't attempted to stop that evening's arrangements for Merida, but of course, to try to stop Merida's fun was like trying to stop day turning into night. And so many other things happened.

It was strange. Everything appearing

so completely normal right up to the children's bed-time. They let Susan tuck them in, and heard her go downstairs to sit with Mrs. Boffin until ten. Then Mrs. Boffin said she thought she'd go to bed, so Susan went, but she didn't undress. She stood at the open window looking out into the velvet night, and a sky so twinkling with a mass of stars that she wanted to hold on to the memory. It was all so peaceful. The hum of traffic from the busy roads beyond the old village seemed a long, a comfortably long way away. The church clock chimed the half-hour. A neighbour's cat started a fight with an importunate dog, and someone spoke, saying goodnight to a neighbour. It was all so peaceful that she decided to turn into bed early herself. Except that Merida was still out.

Susan quietly left the bedroom so as not to disturb Elspeth, and decided to go downstairs and read. If she went to bed she would fall asleep, and for no good reason she was uneasy.

Once downstairs, it occurred to her

to tiptoe up the boys' stairs to see if they and Linda were all right.

She couldn't believe it. Their beds were empty. Linda had gone, too. Susan had never been so frightened in her life. She ran along to Mrs. Boffin's room. The housekeeper was just in bed, in the act of turning off her light. She wasn't pleased.

'Now you look here, I need my sleep! What good can I do, you tell me that! Well, this settles it, doesn't it? Out you all go tomorrow, and if that uncle of yours doesn't like it, he can find someone else to caretake in this place, but I'll have no more of it. Not a minute's peace since you all came, that I haven't had. Go and wake Dinning up!'

Dinning was awake and dressed. 'They've gone to the woods. I heard them say so as they went.'

'Why didn't you stop them?' Susan said wrathfully.

Alf Dinning went on calmly collecting things; a dark pullover which he struggled into, and a very powerful torch. Some rope, and other things. 'What are you doing?' Susan gasped.

'I'm going to get some help,' Dinning said. 'They had a lot of other kids with them and they're up to mischief good and proper tonight. It was no use trying to stop that lot — they had a good start and I was in my bed. But I've got an idea what they're up to and I'm going to put a stop to it, before there's trouble.'

'All right, what can I do?' Susan was suddenly grateful.

'If I was you, I'd go and knock up the doctor,' Alf Dinning said. His eyes were shrewd, but suddenly kind. 'It makes no difference now, lass. You can't do him any more harm, but he might be needed, his services, I mean.'

She didn't stop to think over what he meant. She ran. As she ran, she was aware that the Square was no longer deserted. Other people were about, and some were making towards the woods, but no one spoke to her.

She remembered banging on Gerald

Adams' door. There was a light in the study. It streamed out into the hall, lit the frosted glass of the front door. She heard Gerald's footsteps, hurrying. He threw open the door.

'Susan! Is anything wrong?' He pulled her inside, shut the door and took her by the shoulders. 'You look terrible! My dear, what is it?'

'It's the children — they're out again. And Alf Dinning knew — he was getting ready! He said a lot of them were going and he knows what they're up to and he's taking a rope and tools and — he said I was to fetch you.'

'Take it easy, my dear,' he said, and briefly held her to him. She was so upset, and this seemed such a strange night, that that little action didn't seem at all out of place. She briefly clung to him, her face pressed into his coat. It was the rough tweed of it that brought her to her senses. He normally wore a formal lounge suit, and didn't change in the evenings unless he was dining out. She drew back and looked at it. He had on a thick sweater with a polo collar, too.

'You were going out?' she whispered.

'Yes. To the woods. I've had a rather curious telephone message from Robert Hibbs. This might explain it — your kids, I mean, but somehow I don't think so. Susan, you go back to the house and stay with Elspeth — '

'No, I'm coming too. I must!' she said distractedly.

'All right. Then let's get going.' He, too, had gathered a few things, besides his bag. A huge torch. Susan remembered last time that they were without light of any kind.

Yet when they reached the nearest point of the woods, the spot where the children usually burst their way through the enclosing fence, it all seemed very quiet. Not a light to be seen, not a sound, and at first they couldn't even see the gap in the boundary fence. Gerald, smiling broadly, explained. 'The children have been professional. They brought some tools along and cut a piece, and marked it. Look,' and he pushed back a bush with his foot and pressed against the fence. It swung in.

'Oh, not Frankie and Colin?' Susan protested, and he shook his head. No, it would be the Stogdens, the boys who lived here and had a long-term interest in trespassing.

'I have to meet Hibbs at a given point,' Gerald Adams said. He played his torch on the ground before them, shielding the beam with one hand. Susan followed, her heart thumping painfully. There was a conviction in her that this would be the last night they would be out together looking for the children. She was sure that Mrs. Boffin would have no more of it, even if it cost her her job. What did she care, anyway? It was in the air that she and Alf Dinning were going to be quietly married. But it meant a lot to Susan and the children — the long, long summer holidays weren't yet over.

She suddenly thought, 'Alf Dinning didn't tell me where we were to meet!'

She said it, in a hushed voice in Gerald's ear.

He had stopped. Two people loomed up ahead. Gerald put his torch out and listened, but it wasn't Alf Dinning or Robert Hibbs. It was a stranger, and a girl — a girl in slacks, sweater and something round her head so that at first it had the close-cropped appearance of a man's until the moon was suddenly uncovered and a shaft of light appeared. It was Iris Travers. No doubt about it when she spoke.

'I didn't give you the story because I wanted you to see for yourself! You wouldn't have believed it! Well, now's your chance. It's tonight, and you can take my word for it!'

'I think I'd feel more convinced if the chappie weren't your own uncle, love,' the man drawled, with a hint of amusement in his voice.

'If you don't want the story, I know someone else who does,' she said shortly, and they melted away into the darkness.

Susan looked up at Gerald's face. It was a study, but in the uncertain light she couldn't see anger, nor even surprise and he hadn't even attempted to speak to Iris. He was hanging on to Susan's arm as if he were afraid she, too, would melt away into the darkness.

'Who was that man?' Susan whispered, but Gerald never got an answer framed to that one, for people came threshing through the woods, and he shot forward to meet them. Robert Hibbs was one of them. He was holding one arm. There was a dark stain on one sleeve. 'It's nothing, only a flesh wound,' he said shortly, when Gerald made a move to look at it. 'Never mind this — come with me. Frenwick's dead!'

Frenwick, the man the children had been discussing, the man who had been convicted for a local country house burglary and the haul of silver had never been discovered. Susan felt a little sick. The children would be involved in this, she was sure. Into her mind came

Frankie's voice, earlier that day, in the garden. It had floated in through an open window. Frankie couldn't keep that piping young voice of his down. 'He's digging up the woods! We must see what he's looking for!'

Frenwick digging up the woods, to find the haul he had buried there so long before. It fitted, didn't it? They were going to carve up the woods for a new housing estate and if he didn't work fast, it would be discovered before he got there! She remembered what Joan had said about it, and all the time she hurried to keep up with the men, she wanted to cry out, 'Let me pull the children out of this! Don't let them be involved!'

But they were involved, all seven of them. Linda as well as the two boys; Dickie Stogden and his brother; his friend the policeman's nephew; the police sergeant's boy. Susan realized it with her first sight of them. They weren't all together, and it wasn't until Susan realized this that her worst fears clamped down on her. Frankie was missing, and so was Alf Dinning.

This was a new development that Robert Hibbs didn't know about. He was using this patch of the woods as a short cut to get the body of Frenwick, and as he went, he said shortly and concisely what had happened. 'It was an accident. The most tomfool accident that could have happened and it's burst the whole thing wide open into the light of day. A bit of string across the path. He caught his foot in it and it threw him — hit his head on a bole of a tree. Broke his neck, of course. And we were all trying to keep the thing so quiet.'

Gerald was being borne along with the men. Susan didn't wait to hear any more of that. It would be Frankie's string trap he had learned from Dickie Stogden. She had heard him talking about that. She broke away from Gerald to go back to where the children were, because in the darkness, they had been clustered round a hole, hardly aware of the passing of the intent and anxious adults led by Robert Hibbs. Certainly unaware that a man lay dead through their sinister play.

The group were thoroughly upset. Dickie Stogden saw her. 'It's your Frankie — Mick's terrier went down the foxhole and got stuck and your Frankie went in after her!' he sobbed. He didn't know he was crying, but he was a country child as well as a child of the streets. A curious mixture that gave him knowledge of both the seedy and the harsh world of the woods. He knew, and he said so, between gasps, that any attempt to get Frankie out would bring an earth-fall.

Susan was frantic. She ran back to where the men were moving Frenwick. 'Never mind that! There's a child trapped in a foxhole!' She heard her own voice cut sharply above the whispered voices of the men. They hushed her and she was shocked, swayed by the imperative need for haste where a child's life was concerned. Gerald took her arm and hurried her away.

'Susan, I'll come, but keep your voice down, my dear!' he urged. 'Don't you see, that chap with Iris was from the press.'

'Do you think I care?' Susan panted. 'Frankie — '

'Well, what's done is done,' Gerald said incomprehensibly.

'Let's see about that child!'

For Susan the next fifteen minutes were the worst in her life, and she was powerless to do anything. Robert Hibbs' men brought picks and shovels, and dug out boy and dog, but the drama and the fear were heightened because they all were so intent on being quiet.

'But why, why?' Susan asked, in bewilderment.

Robert Hibbs, standing by her, said, over her head, to Dr. Adams, who had paused to take off his coat and go in to be the first to reach Frankie when they got him out, 'I'd better tell her!'

Gerald Adams nodded, and went back to the men with the pick-axes. Robert Hibbs said very quietly, 'I could wish, my dear, that that uncle of yours hadn't decided to send you all here, this summer of all times!'

'But why?' she said again.

'Because you and those children have two dangerous qualities, so far as I am concerned. You are all so blazingly good that you can't see wrong, or tolerate it if you can, and you're all so inquisitive.'

Susan winced. 'I'm sorry about the children but — '

'It doesn't help, my dear. Frenwick, poor devil, had remission of his sentence for good behaviour and came here to join my little lot, and he was left alone. It would have been (or should have been) easy for him to work in peace, looking for where he hid the stuff!'

'But that's wicked! You surely weren't going to let — ' Susan began indignantly.

'There you go again! Without knowing all the details you are ready to condemn! I wanted him to find it, and let me go through it before we turned it over to the police because there was something there that belonged to me.'

'But the police would have given it to you!'

He sighed. 'Not without the whole world hearing about it which was the last thing I wanted. It was a letter in a quite exquisitely-wrought silver trinket box. A letter which had no harm in it when it was written, but if exposed now, all these years afterwards, wouldn't do me or the lady any good.'

Susan's silence spoke for itself. 'All right,' Robert Hibbs said with resignation, 'You are prejudging again. All right, I admit it, it was indiscreet of me at the time and not entirely ethical the way I've gone about retrieving it. But it had been written to the wife of a local person of importance — '

Susan remembered where the haul had been taken from. She said aloud, 'Jotham Court — Peregrine's aunt?'

'Oh, yes, Peregrine Jotham! I had as much to fear from that young man, too. Did you know he was on a newspaper?'

'That was Peregrine talking to Iris in the woods not long ago?' Susan gasped.

'Oh, but of course! I thought the voice — '

Now it all began to fit in. She stood there, half-watching the men, who seemed to be getting Frankie out at last. She had no will to go to him, she was so angry with him. She could see he was standing up, trying to quieten the yapping of the dog he had gone to save. The children were all churning round him, held back by the doctor and the men. Frankie was talking as usual and being very excitable. Later she would go to him, when her anger had cooled, but for the moment she was split in two, seeing the dilemma of the adults, all their fears and desires and little plans, ruined by a child like Frankie and his friends, who were so sure that life was full of adventure and just for them to unravel, regardless.

Quite suddenly Susan saw what a pitiful lot these adults were, in their attempts to take the law in their own hands and not to bend it too much. Inkpen, trying to hide the one mistake he had made in his life, without knowing that Joan was aware of it. Robert Hibbs holding Inkpen off from pushing a deal through that would tear up the woods, before he had found the one bit of evidence of the one stupid thing he had done in his life — a young man's indiscreet letter! Mrs. Boffin must have known some of it, or guessed — from Alf Dinning, who was reputed to poach sometimes. Secrets, and everyone knew or guessed, yet they all believed that their own particular bit of a secret was safe.

Gerald Adams came over to her and took her by the arms. 'Susan, where's Hibbs?' and she said, without thinking, 'You got Frankie out safely. Oh, Gerald!' and dipped her head against his shoulder. Indiscreet, indiscreet, the word hammered in her head. He doesn't belong to you — get away from him! But she couldn't. She was beaten. This night would decide Uncle Damien.

But the nightmare of it wasn't finished. Gerald still wanted to know where

Robert Hibbs was. 'He went,' she said. 'He went, I think, when I said Iris had been talking to Peregrine Jotham. Oh!' she said, remembering something else. 'Then if Peregrine was here in the woods with her, who is Merida out with?'

'Susan, *darling*,' Gerald Adams said, with an intensity of feeling she couldn't decide was anger or not, 'I don't care about Merida or those little horrors of kids over there — all I want is Robert Hibbs. Your Frankie has found his box!'

He thrust her away from him and spoke to one of the other men, and they fanned out to find Robert Hibbs. Frankie hurled himself at Susan. 'Isn't it super? We found the robbers' haul before the coppers got here — Dickie's friend's uncle and his sergeant are in the woods and we found it first!'

A man had died, and the reputation of another was about to collapse in shreds through the games of these children, Susan thought, and despair loosened her angry tongue. 'Frankie, do you realize what you've done? I told you not to come out at night! You disobeyed me! You've done a terrible thing! You had no business to touch that box!'

'But that ole prisoner was digging it up — he was going to take it away but we put it in the foxhole for the police! That's why Mick went in — he's only a little dog and he thought it was hides, for him to dig out! Gosh Susan — '

'Frankie, you've all done a terrible thing!' she said again, and Frankie fell back, abashed before the way she was looking at them.

And then suddenly the peace of the woods was again shattered. This time by a shout, a girl's scream, and the scream of tyres, from the secondary road that cut through the back of the woods. Susan waited the split second, and there was the crash. She had heard something like that before, but it hadn't concerned her personally. Now she had a terrible feeling that it did, and as always when Merida was out, Susan was afraid for her.

She said to Frankie and the others, 'Stay with Alf Dinning! Don't dare, after what you've all done tonight, don't dare move!' and she ran in the wake of the other men, using her open torch beam now. It didn't matter. They weren't taking precautions any more. Whatever it was, it no longer mattered about caution.

The road lay nearer than she had thought. The two policemen were there on the spot. They had been in that neck of the woods waiting for the children, whom they had been following. There was a car, bonnet crushed against a big old tree that should have been moved long ago because it protruded into the road. A girl passenger hung out of the swinging shattered door, the driver was slumped over the steering wheel. And in the road lay Iris Travers, a shattered press camera beside her.

Robert Hibbs was bending over her. One of his men muttered, 'She was running off so we shouldn't get that chap's camera. Slid down into the road before the car. Couldn't stop herself.'

But Susan wasn't looking at Iris. She couldn't stop staring at the girl passenger. It was Merida.

10

Iris and Merida and her companion were taken to the hospital in Quenning-well. Susan thought she would remember that night all her life. She sat waiting in a starkly clean waiting-room, and she could see herself in the reflection of the plate-glass window; dirty, with twigs in her hair, and a new jagged tear in her sweater. Alf Dinning, who was with her, wasn't much better.

Alf had taken the children home and driven back to the hospital in his second-hand car. He had taken on a new stature this night, helping to dig out the children but mostly in the way he had handled everything. Robert Hibbs' men had gone to pieces at the sight of the police and what had happened to Frenwick, and the fact that Robert himself had gone in another ambulance with a bullet wound in the arm that some of them hadn't known about, had finished them. He had lost a lot of blood and was being kept in overnight.

Susan said to Alf Dinning, 'Where . . . where is Dr. Adams?'

Alf looked quietly pleased, but more amused than anything else. 'He got called out on a case, miss.'

'But . . . I thought no one wanted him any more,' Susan faltered, remembering.

'That's people for you. The Colonel's poor young lady did a good job of spreading scandal around, but when it comes to the crunch and a young wife falls downstairs and the baby's on the way, they know which doctor to call on, scandal or no. He's a good doctor, is Dr. Adams.'

'Yes. Yes, I'm sure he is,' Susan said, unthinking. She kept remembering him in the woods; half-angry, half-frustrated, almost unthinkingly holding her to him in a protective gesture whenever there seemed to be danger. He'd be a good man to look after one for life, she thought.

But she was too numbed to work any of it out. It had been too much, this night, and she couldn't see how she could have prevented it.

'What do you suppose will happen to my cousin Merida?' she managed at last.

Alf Dinning said, after giving it due thought, 'I reckon they'll know soon and they'll come and tell us about all three of 'em. I've seen a few accidents in my time, one way and another. They mostly look worse till they're examined and cleaned up, if you see what I mean.'

He's comforting me, Susan thought in despair. Poor Uncle Damien, what would he think when he heard? 'Oh, someone ought to have told him — my uncle, I mean!'

'Mrs. Boffin did, miss,' Alf Dinning said. 'I told her to get him right away. He'll be coming down here.'

'He'll take us all away,' Susan said flatly.

'Mrs. Boffin's going to put in a word for you all to go to her niece's,' Alf said, in this new comforting way of his. His love affair with Mrs. Boffin certainly seemed to have mellowed him! 'It isn't right,' he went on, 'all that responsibility, on a young girl's shoulders, and you not nineteen yet, miss.' And he looked so kindly at her, Susan felt near tears again.

At that moment a doctor walked in, a ward sister behind him. He was a very good-looking young man. The sister said, 'Miss Vengrove? This is Mr. Wilcock, our R.S.O., and he's come to tell you about your cousin.'

She sounded very severe, but the young man smiled easily and said, 'She'll be all right. I've set her leg, and she's got some beautiful bruises, but she's been lucky. She's healthy, so not to worry. A few days' rest and she'll be bright and perky again.'

'And the others? We knew them, at least, Miss Travers,' Susan faltered.

'Miss Travers didn't get off so lightly, but she'll be all right, given time,' he said. 'What about Miss Vengrove's father? Is he coming?'

Alf Dinning said he would be, and after that he took Susan home. Back from that stark, clean, cold-looking efficient place where girls no older than she moved coolly about, unruffled at things going on such as Merida's accident . . .

Susan lay wondering what Uncle Damien would say. Elspeth had heard the story from the boys and had been as thrilled yet unaffected by the drama of it, as they had been. Sometimes Elspeth seemed so grown-up, yet at other times she was just eleven, perfectly normal, dividing the world into 'goods' and 'bads'. Susan fell asleep wondering what would be best for the children — for her to stay with them or to leave them in Mrs. Boffin's care and later to the care of the boarding-schools her uncle would choose for them. Was she good for them or not?

Uncle Damien, Susan found, was affected in quite a different way than she had expected. Instead of being irritated to find his time was being cut into by any nonsense from the children, he was deeply shocked by the first sight of Merida, and he remained so.

Merida was asleep when he was shown into her private room. There were one or two scratches on her forehead, but mostly her face was untouched and she had never looked so lovely, Susan thought. Her blonde hair was splayed all over the pillows. The nurses kept tying it neatly into bunches but somehow those ribbons kept vanishing. There was a tender, vulnerable air about her that the R.S.O., standing behind Uncle Damien with the ward sister, found rather startling. Susan saw with a smile that he, too, was very much affected by Merida's loveliness.

But poor Uncle Damien could only say, in a hushed voice very much like his own, 'She looks just like her mother, before she died.' And nothing could convince him that Merida was going to recover and quite reasonably quickly.

He stayed almost a week at The White House. In that time he not only heard the full story but there was a lot more to recount than Susan had discovered on that dreadful night in the woods. 'Am I to understand,' Uncle Damien demanded, 'that this chemist fella was rigging up cameras in the woods ostensibly to record nature but really to catch anyone doing what they shouldn't, so he could use it against them to get himself out of a mess?' Uncle Damien couldn't believe that anything could be wrong under the surface of a place like Holland Green.

Susan gently assured him that that was more or less true. 'It seems he heard that Iris Travers was meeting Peregrine there, to give him her uncle's secret. It wasn't for the money for the story, so much as to get even with her uncle because he insisted on holding back her inheritance. He was one of the trustees and he didn't feel she should have it all to squander and there was a clause that gave him freedom to hold back the bulk of it till he was satisfied.'

'But bless me, I thought that was the girl who was engaged to this doctor fella — Adams!'

Susan's colour heightened. 'Well, she was, but it seems that Gerald — I mean, Dr. Adams, didn't feel they ought to go on. She made it clear she didn't want to stay here in Holland Green and he did!' That was all Susan had been told and she didn't want to talk about it.

Damien Vengrove got the rest of the story from other people. The vicar, distressed as he was over the whole thing, was as willing to talk as everyone else and probably knew a great deal more. 'Poor girl, she never did understand that she couldn't pressure people to get her own way,' he said, shaking his head. 'It appears that she told Dr. Adams she wasn't going to release him when he wanted to. You do know, of course, well, it's an open secret, that he and your niece — well, perhaps I shouldn't say this, but I can't help feeling (and my wife joins me in this) that she would make a far better local G.P.'s wife than the Colonel's daughter! Anyway, he's taking her on a cruise. She'll get over it I'm sure. She'll find someone else who joins her in her dislike of a life in Holland Green. Personally I can't imagine why anyone wants to leave it — terribly interesting place!'

Uncle Damien didn't share his view. 'Bless my soul, I only sent my daughter and niece down here with the children for nine miserable weeks' summer holiday, and look what's happened! It sounds like one of those ghastly boys' magazine things Colin is always stuffing his head with! They're at the bottom of it, I'm sure! Burglars' hauls buried in the woods, indeed, and children getting caught down foxholes, to say nothing of cameras and secrets — '

The vicar smiled sadly. 'We read about such things in our Sunday papers, my dear sir, but it's always in someone else's part of the countryside, never in our own small corner. When we get involved, we are always so angry that it should happen to us. Ah, well, all the excitement is over now, I should imagine. The police got their hands on the box of stolen things and poor Hibbs has packed up and gone away and I doubt if he'll come back, and I hear that the owners of Jotham Court are selling out and going away, too. Perhaps something good will come of it, after all.'

Uncle Damien was quite sure it wouldn't. He said he was going to put The White House on the market, as soon as he could and take the family back home with him, to be despatched to their respective schools. Merida was to go to a finishing school after she had recuperated, and his only problem was what to do with Susan.

Meantime, Mrs. Boffin was going to take them all to her young relative, and Uncle Damien, who had had business problems looming large in his absence, was glad enough to go back to London and shake the dust of Holland Green off his feet for ever.

The night before they were to go, Susan was returning from seeing Merida in the hospital, and was just getting off the bus when Dr. Adams stopped her. He was returning from bringing yet another baby into the world of Holland Green.

'Will you get in, Susan, and let me drive you around for a few minutes? I want to talk to you, and I hear that Mrs. Boffin will be carrying you off tomorrow while I'm in surgery.' He added smilingly, 'It's all right. No one cares about me giving you lifts now Iris no longer wants me.'

Susan got in beside him, wishing she could have avoided this. He still had the power to put her in a ferment of excitement, and he didn't seem to notice it.

'I can't talk while driving,' he said. 'There's a quiet spot I know, with a view.'

She reflected that it didn't matter much now. She was going away tomorrow. She said, 'Did I cause you and Miss Travers to fall out? You were engaged to be married, and everyone else was peaceful, when we came, and we messed it all up.'

'I can't speak for other people, my dear, but I personally was very glad you came. You see, when two people meet at a party (well, a do at the vicarage, actually) they are automatically on their best behaviour. That's how Iris and I were, all the time. Formally engaged and behaving formally. I never had the chance to see her with her back hair down, as I saw you. I've seen you doing comfortable things for Elspeth in the sickroom, and I've seen you coping with a crowd of children at a fair. I've seen you torn with anxiety, running through dark woods in search of three tiresome children who should have been in bed. I think I've only seen you on occasions when most young women wouldn't have wanted to be seen — and I've liked what I saw.'

He groped for and found her hand and kept on holding it. 'I think if I'd seen poor Iris as she was, struggling with her father about keeping her uncle's poor little secret, and struggling with her uncle over the matter of the legacy, and skilfully starting little rumours because she was bored to tears with this district — she looked so lovely I would never have believed it. Until I was forced to accept the truth of it.'

'You mean, on that night in the woods?'

'No, before then, when she made it clear that she wanted me out of my job here in Holland Green, and that she wasn't very particular what methods she used to get her own way.'

'Well, it's all over now.'

'What will you do, Susan, when the children go to school and Merida goes abroad to her finishing school? That's what I really wanted to ask you.'

'I don't know. I hope it means you've got a job in sight for me. I could do with some suggestions. Only . . . I know now, after being at the hospital, that I couldn't be a nurse. They all looked so impersonal and that's as it should be. I don't think that's for me. I want to be with children — well, any home nursing, I don't mind that, but I want to be with children, and somewhere where I can feel I'm some use to people. It's been such a chastening experience, this holiday in Holland Green. I've felt I haven't been of any use to anyone.'

'You know that's not true, my dear. There's Elspeth and the other children who have a lot to thank you for, and, in an odd way, I think everyone will feel better for your being here, because though you may not have meant to do it, by just being yourself, it's brought it all out into the open and that was needed, badly. If I offered you something in Holland Green, could you bear to accept it? Could you bear to go on living here, perhaps for always?'

'Holland Green!' She thought about it. 'What will it be like, with Robert Hibbs gone for good, and no prisoners, and Yoxbrook Manor closed up again, and yes, The White House sold?'

'It might be rather nice. There are certainly possibilities,' he said cheerfully. 'I have it on good authority that Yoxbrook will probably be turned into a holiday centre, because of the Creek. And the woods will almost certainly be developed. There'll be a lot more work for me, and I could do with help.'

'You mean you want me to help you?' she said uncertainly.

'Yes, in a way. My dear, can't you see? I'm asking you to marry me! I don't know how I dare, really, I'm so hard up and I probably never will have enough money for everything. But Susan, I love you very much, my dear. Dear Susan, you're my kind of woman, and I didn't realize it until you came back, surrounded by children; almost covered up in one of Mrs. Boffin's aprons you stood there, and you looked me in the eyes and all of a sudden I knew how all wrong it was to be engaged to anyone else to be married. It was only you, my dear. Only you.'

She found herself in his arms, and he

was smoothing her hair back from her face. 'Susan, you're going away tonight. Will you come back to me when the children go back to school?'

'Come back to you,' she repeated. 'Oh, Gerald, how nice that sounds. That's what I felt when I knew we were coming to Holland Green for these summer holidays . . . going back to the Holiday Doctor,' and she put her face up to his and he kissed her. A long, satisfying kiss.

She nestled her head against his cheek and thought about it, savouring it. For the first time for such a long, long time, she felt she belonged to someone. Here in Holland Green, as the doctor's wife, she would count. Everyone would be her friend, and he had said she was his kind of woman. 'Oh, yes, Gerald, and you're my kind of man.' She sighed with sheer happiness. 'I'll come back to you, Gerald, for always.'

We do hope that you have enjoyed reading this large print book.

Did you know that all of our titles are available for purchase?

We publish a wide range of high quality large print books including:
Romances, Mysteries, Classics
General Fiction
Non Fiction and Westerns

Special interest titles available in large print are:
The Little Oxford Dictionary
Music Book, Song Book
Hymn Book, Service Book

Also available from us courtesy of Oxford University Press:
Young Readers' Dictionary
(large print edition)
Young Readers' Thesaurus
(large print edition)

For further information or a free brochure, please contact us at:
Ulverscroft Large Print Books Ltd.,
The Green, Bradgate Road, Anstey,
Leicester, LE7 7FU, England.
Tel: (00 44) **0116 236 4325**
Fax: (00 44) **0116 234 0205**

MYSTERY AT MORWENNA BAY

Christina Garbutt

Budding criminologist Ellie is glad to help her gran recuperate after an accident, expecting to spend a quiet month in rural Wales before heading back to London to submit her PhD. But she's bemused to find that she's something of a celebrity in the village, and expected to help solve a series of devastating livestock thefts for which there is no shortage of suspects. She's also wrong-footed by the friendly overtures of handsome young farmer Tom — even though a relationship is absolutely the last thing she wants or needs . . .

JEMIMA'S NOBLEMAN

Anne Holman

1816: When her father's famous fan shop in the Strand is reduced to ashes, Jemima dons the clothing of a maid and moves with him to the docklands of London — and is present at an accident where William, Earl of Swanington, almost literally falls into her lap! But William is fleeing from accusations that he's murdered a servant — and when he sees the beautiful Jemima at a Society ball, he wonders if she's the one who robbed him after his accident! Can true love blossom in such circumstances?